D0221626

How Strange It Is To Be Anything At All

First edition, February 2012
Copyright © 2012 Word Palace Press
wordtemplepress.com
wordtemplepress@aol.com

Word Palace Press
P.O. Box 583
San Luis Obispo, CA 93406

BOOK AND COVER DESIGN BY
Ben Lawless, Penciled In Design
penciledin.com

COVER ILLUSTRATIONS BY
Ina Mar
ina-mar.com

ISBN: 0985026006
ISBN-13:   978-0-9850260-0-4
LIBRARY OF CONGRESS CONTROL NUMBER:
              2012933806

HOW STRANGE IT IS TO BE ANYTHING AT ALL

STORIES BY JOE RILEY

CONTENTS

Dedicated to: Mom, David, and Jessie.

These are the people that inspired me to get my shit together for five minutes at different points.

Thank you.

AUTHOR'S NOTE

This book isn't about addiction. It's not about love, death, or taxes. It's about confusion in relation to everything said above. It's about learning how to accept that this confusion is part of living, and that destiny is predicated upon what you want.

It's about neither fate nor faith, but understanding that they are the same thing, and you shouldn't believe in either.

But really it's about being grateful to exist. It's about appreciating life because you don't have to walk 20 miles for fresh water. About being able to go out at night without the fear of being snatched by a 30 foot Anaconda.

It's about understanding that without all this fucked up chaos there could never be irrepressible beauty, and understanding that you can't understand.

HOW
STRANGE
IT IS

TO BE
ANYTHING
AT ALL

WHITE LIGHTS
IN A **HOSPITAL**

I can feel the blood running down my chin and neck, forming an incredibly shallow pool below my adam's apple at the peak of my chest. What happened? My neck tightens and my vain attempt to rotate it is respectfully denied by the bracing safety of an ambulance stretcher.

But the sirens aren't blaring and words are silk echoes laced with laughter. The laughter directed towards me, but why? Why these damn bands around my wrists, this horrible claustrophobia tunneling my vision, and the strategic placing of my head, strapped far too tight, overwhelming what could barely be considered a thought process. I need to get out.

I shout belligerent obscenities, the big 2 included. These nonsensical ramblings are indeci-

pherable, and the only effect they serve is as an-
noyance to my licensed chaperones. There's no
resisting on this path to I don't know where, from
I don't know what: why am I wearing two different color socks? Which gives rise to the question
of the location of my shoes. An interesting story
unto itself, I'm sure, but unfortunately sobriety is
returning and with no subtle respect to my dam-
aged senses. The only thing I am able to focus on
is the horrible burning sensation coming from
my lips.

Bisected by broken teeth looking like piano
keys from the pen of Tex Avery.

The ambulance chugs along, not close
enough to the road for my situation to be urgent.
Then the mobile stops, backdoors fly open, and
the sideways shit-faced grins of the EMT's turn
Chicago Hope with the speed of my stretcher
flying towards the white light. First rule of Tex
Avery: white light=death.

The wheels ride smooth on the slick lino-
leum; I'm still flustered as hell and have no idea
what's going on. They roll me with unnecessary
speed into what looks like a storage closet. An
MD with another shit eating grin leans over me
with condescension and talks real slow like I can't

understand the language. The Sesame Street display continues until I get the words out for him to fuck off. His mouth drops open, sorry junior life isn't what it was supposed to be.

My arms are still bound—if there were some leather, some spikes, maybe a whip involved this could be fun, but I'm pretty sure you're not supposed to have fun at times like these.

Several male nurses stroll in, eerily smiling. Why all the smiles, maybe they're trying to look good for death? At this point I wish I could say the pain had resided. But, life doesn't work like that, the burning still hurt a shitload, and I have no idea about the current condition of my face. I decide I'll need to be decent to get any freedom in this joint; all an hour of no compliance has gotten me is an itchy nut sack.

—"Are you going to cooperate now?"

—"Release my hands and I'll be good."

No go. They walk out of the room, and I figure I got at least an hour to kill. One thought still pleases me; pissing all over the stretcher would be extremely punk rock.

As the earth slowly spins, my mind starts piecing together the hole in my face, or at least its origin. I was with my people at one point.

And we were drinking. We drank a lot. Car rides, several stops, and a few bad choices later, I'm facedown on the asphalt equally warm from the recently set sun and my newly introduced blood. I know I fell, by no fault of anyone else, but I don't know how I know. It's like my subconscious put my soul in the third person, and I hopelessly watched self-mutilation. Top lip, broken tooth, with a nose to follow: bam, right on the curb. The broken tooth is the part I want to think about least. The facial contact of my bone to the dirty flat asphalt, with momentum, makes me not want to think about the sound that followed. Like nails on a chalkboard inside your brain, and the duration of the sound was an insult to the extremity of its reverberated sensation. The shit felt like turbulence on Air U.S.S.R.

Pieces of my mind slowly return to me. I have an address and a job. A favorite TV show and a record player. I like to go out drinking, I like smoking, and women can be described as one of my weaknesses. I forget people's birthdays, their names, and I'm perpetually 6 minutes late. I call my mom when I'm bored, usually while walking alone, and tell her little things that my friends would never care about; she cares.

The henchmen come back, looking like pa-
tients given the responsibility of their own mental
health. Same questions as before, and this time I
cooperate: arbitrary bullshit to escape from the
broom closet. My first victory of the night. The
doctors come, they go. My inebriation is in, is
out, coming, going, usually gone while I sit idly
in pain, then resurfacing (Praise Bacchus!) when
I need it most. Moment to moment it helps me
escape this consuming claustrophobia that has
been the past 3 hours of my life. Arms bound,
neck tied, helpless like a newborn.

After finally balancing the seesaw inebriation,
I get my arms released as a reward for good be-
havior. They feel light. I touch my face and feel
its tarnished scape. I feel my tooth, or where part
of my tooth use to be, it's sharp. They show me a
mirror. I start to cry. I don't know why, it doesn't
hurt that bad, but I start to cry. I can't stop. It
makes me feel better.

The inhumane insanity of the drone like
guards has dissipated, and they become human
support, an audience for my tears. After the tears,
the inebriation steadies, still obvious, especially in
the observance of my thought process, but lucid
enough for the questioning to begin.

—"Who are you, where do *you* live, how old are *you*?"

Too much. No answers, the cascade of questions grounds me in reality. Before this, this could have all been one big beautiful horrible dream.

—"Where's your insurance, who's your emergency contact, are you listening?!?"

After half answering half the questions, I demand the sanctuary of a cigarette and 5 minutes to myself. The answer is swiftly and undeniably, "No."

"What's your mother's maiden name? At what age did you learn to read? Is Pluto still a planet?"

—"Cigarette. Please, cigarette. Cigarette please."

—"No, not a chance. Absolutely not."

More questions. Always three, no allotted time to answer.

—"What's your birthday, do you have any allergies, what kind of pants are you wearing?"

For fuck sakes, shut up! Please Please Please. I need to get out of here, from these white coats and teeth, the mousse in their hair. FOR!! Fucks Sake, let me have my five minutes of mourning for my face, and myself, and my life. And then I'll sign the damn papers. OKAY.

Still not a chance. I tried, I guess that's good enough. I give in. Completely defeated, wrist limp with shame. Paper, after paper, after paper, same signature, same spot, same wording with different words.

—"Doesn't the fact that I, drunk, make these signatures nullified?"

—

No answer, next paper. I tried. More questions that now have become seasoning on cold excrement leftovers. All I care about now is being released from this building. For all I know, this is the only building in existence. And if I died when my face hit the asphalt with such serious impact, this most definitely could be my horrible self-involved idea of hell. Bright lights, cold walls, decrepit sad men sitting on neglected chairs, their heads in their hands. And the sick women, with their sick children crying in the sick night, in the lobby of a sick, public hospital. Hell or no hell, this is hell.

Then, without explanation, I am set free! Not just my arms, but my feet, and my soul. Walking the streets again (yes they still exist). But where the *fuck* am I? How am I going to get home? The real problems return while the seemingly surreal problems stay put, like the gash on my face. But who gives a fuck, I just want a cigarette, and then I'll let reality run. I open-palm tap my pocket. There is my wallet, and phone, but no pack of sweet synthetic death.

I flag down a cab: the driver's middle-eastern, just being honest, sometimes stereotypes are what they're made of. He refuses to drive me, due to the cartoonish amount of dried blood on my face, on my shirt, some wet, some dry. He doesn't want to get his cab dirty.

—"Do you at least have a cigarette!?"

He drives hastily away.

A man pulls up right after him, in a black sedan. He is of some sort of ethnicity, this I am sure. He offers to give me a ride, I graciously accept. This whole nightmarish life cul-de-sac will soon be done and gone forever. Toward the end of the brief ride, I ask if he has a cigarette, he doesn't. I give him far too much money; step out of his far too nice car, and onto my driveway. A drop of blood falls from my nose, passing directly by my stitched up lip and broken tooth, finding a spot on the concrete to forever call its own, a smoothly round red spot of myself.

I step into my house and immediately see two of my friends, still high on ecstasy, and ask them the time. They answer; much earlier than I thought it was. They say the night was amazing, too bad I couldn't make it, holy shit your face looks like death.

—"Give me a goddamn cigarette."

They hastily comply; this is what friends are for. It's a menthol. I'm too disheveled, humbled, shitty-blasted by the world to care. I smoke it slow and fast. It was worth the wait. I think there are probably negative effects of having smoke re-peatedly pass over an open wound on your face: I don't care, continuing to smoke.

I wake up the next morning. A girl in my bed. She looks at me as she wakes up crying.

The next night at a party, where I am fool-ishly drinking again, I receive comments from girls about how handsome I use to be. This makes me feel strangely good and immovably sad, will I look like this forever?

The only strange part of the night is the stares fixated too long to not notice them. Where my eyes meet theirs, I can see the question, but they're too afraid to ask, so they quickly shoot their eyes away; only at these times am I aware of the death on my face.

—

I tried acid for the first time several months later. There I was, my face healed, lying on my back in a field, in a city, smiling. The vertical expanse of the universe seemed endless; horizons clashing to create the sunset, stars blinking for me, and me for them, sparkling like the glorious eyes of the young girl you first cherished. Then it was dark and cold. And I remembered what cell phones were.

After someone who was not me used the voice reciprocator, a car arrived, and morphed us home, lefts disappearing and rights transposing themselves through the course of the wheels. Somehow I was safe. I sat laughing in my garage, insane hysterics of nothing, my stomach curdling from the hysteria and the drugs. I looked down, a breath between laughs, and saw a piece of mail.

My name is on it. It was from the public hospital that stitched up my face: a bill. Life has a horrible tendency to follow you wherever you go.

The acid settled and real life started squeezing, prying itself with the careless sympathy of a much-used crowbar, rubbing itself sweetly where it pleases. Then sad spiky rain running like hungry dogs on a frictionless track, downward into broken piles of unyielding emotion. Second time I've cried that month, and the tears hitting the ground returned to me, slowly, the pieces of my mind.

HATE
EVERYTHING

The following is a comprehensive (but not complete) list of absolutely everybody it is acceptable to hate. Note: this list is susceptible to addition but never subtraction.

You should hate the jocks, the cheerleaders, the sluts, the prudes, the ever-too-eager over achievers, the stoners, and those who pack snaps when there are more than two people. Don't forget the too drunk, the too dumb, and the too neutral to stand out, and so after meeting them for the tenth time, you still don't know their name.

Hate those who leave their blinkers on, those who don't use blinkers at all. The condescending, the far too intrigued, the music snobs, the bike snobs, those hubris stroking *piece of shit literature snobs*. Hate your grocer, your postmaster, the local head of the PTA, the pigs, the feds, but most of all those fucking meter maids with the flitzy helmets. Hate it when people use the f word followed by an 'a,' not a 'u,' when they take politics too seriously; and you should certainly never trust someone who voluntarily drinks Pepsi before Coke.

Always be wary of those who don't curse, those who don't dance, though there are notable exceptions depending on your BAC (or your B[MDM]AC), those who don't dance, then drink, then drive, then fly off a fucking cliff or into a street light, disconcerted but level, the only damper of their otherwise enjoyable night being the bisected corpse between the metal of their grill and the mangled form of a streetlight, hanging like a puppet, intestines like strings. For humanities' sake please hate the potentially 3RD world country saving amounts of money they will spend on keeping themselves out of jail.

Hate the football fans, the baseball fans, those in favor of Coors, NASCAR, and America synergizing into the ultimate 4TH of July Wet Dream Corporation. Hate the cynical barflies, the bitchy barmaids, and the over-weight (paid) servers with their prickish goatees. Hate those who don't tip, talk, and use an elevator when they could just as easily take the stairs (levels 4 and over excluded, of course). Hate the insurance salesmen, the wall-street monkey-suit morons, and the agenda push-ers—which includes everyone on Capitol Hill, regardless of race, color, or gender because we're a land that believes in equivocation.

Condemn those afraid to speak their mind, those who can't make up their mind, the sheep, the pawns, the armadillos and all other high school mascots. Hate the wine connoisseurs, the ornithologists, the bridge enthusiasts and anyone who drives a yellow car. And while we're on cars anyone that does drive or has driven a Hummer, even if it was only for a test drive.

Hate the girls, the women, the chicks, the smart ones, the dumb ones, the pretty ones, the moderate ones, the pretty moderate ones and ev-erything in-between. Hate the boys, with their arrogance, insecurity and obvious repressed sexual orientations. These orientations being their most unilaterally indicative characteristic, save for the astonishing ability to mark out things that may look like a penis or relate to them.

Hate your brothers, your sisters, your aunts, especially your creepy uncles, maybe your mom, maybe your dad, but really you should never hate both. Hate your house, your town, and what you see when you look in the mirror. Hate the post, the metro, the sun and his lunar mistress. Hate Albert Einstein and his space-time continuum. Hate Adam and Eve for their sins. Hate Abraham for the realization of these sins. Hate Isaac, Joseph, Jesus and that god filled slut Mary.

But please remember never to hate yourself, because, oh how strange it is to be anything at all.

THE GREEN-EYED
MONSTER
OF HAPPINESS

1. JUST ME, JUST HER

The searing pain of realization is as swift and sharp as an icicle wind. The curtains are pulled back to reveal the world for what it truly is—a disgusting pit of conceit and vanity. This is all her fault. THIS IS ALL HER FUCKING FAULT! She sullied my name, reputation and pride. For what? For a kiss. I don't know if it's true or not, but I assume the worst. That's my half-Jewish side, pessimistic. Why did he have to tell me, it was so perfect.

I call her.

—Me: "We need to talk."

There is more urgency in my voice than I would have liked, and it creates a sudden, desperate panic in her.

—Her: "What is it?"

My voice, broken.

—Me: "Just come."

These are the longest fifteen minutes of my life. My brain is wrestling in a free-for-all of frenzied thoughts and forsaken memories. Every bad has a good, every good has a better, and every better has a bitter.

She walks into my room unannounced, but expected all the same. We hug limply, she weary, I stiff. We break, our eyes meet. In this chaos of frenzy, suddenly everything goes blank.

Nothing matters, just me, just her.

Everything's okay. My eyes drift past her towards the window. The pain, anger, and jealousy return as quickly as they left. I hate her! How could she do this? Doesn't she care? Doesn't she give a flying fuck! Her fear grows, I can feel it. Her anxious tension rises to the surface of her skin. Her voice breaks the silence after what feels like a hundred years of aimless wandering through the fields of my mind. She whispers, defeated and vulnerable,

—"Is everything okay?"

Here it comes. I'm going to confront her, crush her, she doesn't stand a chance. I look into her eyes so she can feel my pain. I'm going to destroy her, but when our eyes meet, the pain is gone. I'm left with the sight of those dark chocolate pools, gazing at me. A twinkle of feeling dances perfectly in her eyes. My anger, my jealousy, my pain vanish—it doesn't matter anymore.

Just me. Just her.

I wrap myself around her, she melts into my arms.

—Her (pleading whisper): "Everything okay?"

—Me: "It is now."

After all, it was only a kiss, and nothing else matters, just me, just her.

2. GOOD NIGHT

We'd all been there and seen it before: the placid chaos of ol' Stan Evans' house. Choreographed spontaneity that makes the D.M.V. look like the antithesis of bureaucracy. We all smile, we all laugh, we all put up the front that this is a drugged-out Disneyland, and we act like we're seven; Mickey Mouse doesn't get arrested for spousal abuse, and we don't notice the injustice of Pluto sleeping in a dog house while fellow canine Goofy is allowed to gallivant freely.

Everyone was there; I guess that's why it was boring. Everyone was there, no one was missing, and no one new had arrived. Nobody new, just the same old boring prudes that we pretend to like so our parents and peers don't proclaim us as libertine homosexuals. When they speak, we laugh, we don't listen, we laugh and smile and everything is okay, everything's okay.

There's drinking. Of course there's drinking, everyone drinks; it's like *Rainy Day Woman #12 and #35,* "Everybody must get (insert [chemical] vice of choice here)." There used to be a time when people would drive drunk, stoned, fucked-up, but those days are long gone, packed up in the lunch pails that we exchanged for designer sunglasses. We take cabs now, charge it on our parents' card. But everyone drinks, everyone must drink, and if you don't drink: speculation begins. "Why isn't he/she drinking? They too cool to drink now?" Or the always feared thoughts of inadequacy, the dreaded: "They're not drinking, they're not cool."

Why? Why drinking? Stop for a second and analyze what's actually going on in this delicate process. We're sitting there pouring amber brew down our throats as fast as humanly possible to drown our brains in bitter liquid with a kick. Puts our brains in a pool of inebriation so we can act like idiots, inhibition free. Say stupid things, be sleazy and perverted, and express our love for each other that dissipates in direct correlation with the rising sun.

The main reason everyone drinks is to get laid. We all want to fuck. Girls, guys, everyone. We all want a warm wet feeling. We feel like if we drink, we'll be able to screw and forget. Of course, next day, thoughts of last night yield regret, but that's beside the point, the point is we want to "make love" (fuck).

She's here; she's not everything to everyone, but she's everything to me. I feel her mind like sometimes she lets me feel her breasts. She's beautiful and free. She's smart and wild. She's insanity in a bottle of volatile alcoholism. She's smashed, dancing, hugging, and kissing, while I'm sitting, sulking, and raging. The more fun she has, the drunker I get. Silver aide in hand. Barley taste with promised results. She laughs, I wince. Fortunately, I'm circled by friends, who laugh. We speak but I'm not listening. My eyes fall just past my fellow drunks, my head onto hers. How dare she. Why is she speaking to him? Didn't they date a millennia ago?

Everything you fear and know is going to happen—will. You convince yourself that it won't, the love that you share with the cute girl with the pretty smile won't fade, just because some older guy looks good shirtless. But it will. The friends you shared your childhood with won't fall into a haze of cocaine madness, but they do. You'll never drink and drive, but you will.

I hear her laugh.

The party's the same for hours. Everyone circling around like swimmers in a lap pool, back and forth, having aesthetic conversations with façades of women, caked on faces. They laugh uncomfortably and so do you. You smile. She smiles. He smiles. We are eating the shit radiating from each other's smiles. There's terrible music that sounds the same as the shitty music from the night before. It sounds like Passion Pit and Foster the People being tortured by Gnarls Barkley. It's nice that he tried, Stan. It would have been a pretty quiet Saturday otherwise, but trying and failing is still failing. Never gotten a 'T' before, definitely have gotten an 'F.' But why is she talking to him?

We talk about sports, run out of things to say about sports. We talk about music, run out things to say about this as well. We talk about friends, but are too cautious to admit anything, anything at all. We talk about shit, we talk shit, but all the people we want to talk shit about are right next to us. We laugh, we drink. I think we half keep this charade up for tradition, and keep the other half up because we need the envy of the young ones in our group. Praise is powerful, and we all want some. We want them to feel for us like we did for the older kids when we were their age. We want the younger ones' attention as much as they want ours, we just want it in different ways. They want our acceptance, we want their respect. What in the name of all fucks is she doing, why is she sitting on his lap, is she serious!

The cops always come; they always, always come. Normally before eleven. We lose the beer, but someone who's too drunk to stash it gets a ticket. It's always the same picture, just a different frame. We all leave trying to find a driver, try to find a place to go, to get more fucked-up. We just want more, we always want more, always more. It will work out, we'll just have to drive, we draw straws, who has had the least to drink drives. We've been trying to cut back, because the cops have been raising the stakes; one of our friends got the inevitable first D.U.I., Manuel Michaels. I couldn't believe it, but it makes perfect sense. Everything you know is going to happen does. Where is he? Where is she?

I see a dude I hate, but it's okay, because nobody knows. We speak briefly. Who cares? Who cares? We make plans to do something sometime, and agree we like each other. Who cares? Who cares? We try to laugh, but can't even force it now. Who cares? I see someone else and say the same thing; we always say the same thing. This scene has become so choreographed, it's mindless. She's outside, they're talking.

Suddenly. They all come running, excited— not her. Someone stupid is doing something dumb. We all run outside to witness the moron do something dumb. Jump! Jump! We all want the idiot to jump off the roof. My cheering is especially pathetic. He does. We cheer. YAY, IDIOT! This is automated, we've all seen this a hundred times. She's standing next to him.

Hot girls are the American dream. We all talk about them, and about what we're going to do to them, but very few of us do. It's more fun to talk about it. If our dreams were ever realized, then we wouldn't be able to talk about them anymore. We wander over to some pretty girl with large breasts, they're desperate, we're desperate, we say despicable things in despicable tones, they laugh, we laugh. No respect for them, and none for ourselves, it's OK, though, we're drunk. She's dancing, with him.

The night grinds on. We say we're having fun, but we're not. We try too hard to make everyone think we're having a good time. We say we're individuals, but we are the essence of conformity, there's no difference anymore, everything has become the same under the pressing weight of the desire to be cool. They're too close, I can't stand it.

I reach into my pocket to feel rigid metal on a chain. It's cooling with my heart. I'm drunk. Too drunk. But I can't take it. Not anymore. I'm leaving. I say goodbye. When I say goodbye to her, she acts like nothing's wrong—nothing's wrong! I look at that piece of shit she's standing next to and spit in his face.

Fuck her, fuck me, and especially fuck him. Oh shit. He's popular. Newton dictates this instance will absolutely have an equal and opposite shit storm. But she's drunk, I'm drunk, he's drunk. Maybe nobody saw? No, judging from the uproar and procession of shouting, a large amount of people heard. I decide running is a better idea than walking to my car. Open the door and get in. I'm leaving, for good. Goodbye, Stan. Goodbye, Party. Goodbye, her.

The perfect nightcap to what may be the worst night of my over-privileged life. I smash my 3-series into a palm tree two blocks from my house. A fucking palm tree. If palm trees were people, they'd be those coked out New York whores who suck dick in the back of perverse, half-Goth night clubs, listening to that new New Wave bullshit. It's the skinniest fucking tree and my belligerence careens into one, like it was taking my virginity. In a sense, I suppose it did. That tree, my car, my innocence, maybe my childhood. The real world is not *just* a fucking TV show.

Twenty minutes pass, red and blue lights spinning for America like the dream still exists.

3. LYING IN LOVE

She arrives on time, for once, and lets herself in. This is a bad sign, she never just comes in, she always calls first. Makes me come open the door for her. Girls making boys do shit, birds dancing, same thing. This time, though, I hear her walk down the hall; every step of hers, my heart beats ten. I feel my brain numbing like Novocain on the gums, slow and uncomfortable. I can't think of anything other than the fact that she's about to dump me. I sit in my room trying to imagine the perfect position to be in when she starts talking, crying, shouting, whatever. I decide to lie down on my bed, very nonchalantly pretending like I don't give a damn about anything. This plan is quagmire as soon as I hear her knock.

—Me: "Who is it?"

That was stupid. She doesn't answer, just walks in. She looks drop-dead jaw-to-the-motherfucking-floor beautiful. I miss her already. Her eyes quickly move to a safe corner in my room. This is strictly business. She sits in my computer chair, I take a seat across from her on my bed. She swivels slowly in my direction, facing me.

—Her: "How was your day?"

Wow, she's going to throw down the gauntlet of the monotonous drawl, the formalities, before she tears my heart out. I'd laugh, if I wasn't so nervous.

—Me: "Fine, I went shopping with my mom, and *you know*, did some stuff."

Jesus, how pathetic. I feel like nothing, I'm just too far gone.

She alters her seated position and leans forward.

—Her: "So, how was last night for you?"

Fuck.

—Me: "I don't remember anything, I was extremely intoxicated."

Maybe she's not going to dump me, maybe she just wants to talk? Maybe if I just play dumb, all will be forgiven, and it will all just go away. There is absolutely no fucking way that's going to happen.

—Her: "You don't remember *anything*? *Nothing* at all?"

This is going to be bad, this is going to be a big bad mean motherfucker. I'm not ready to say goodbye, I'm not even ready to say so long for now, or see you later. My pathetic testosterone driving imagination races with delusional thoughts: 'Maybe she'll at least give you a pity fuck.' Testosterone has no shame. And I'm more than fairly certain she can hear my thoughts.

—Me: "Listen, can we go somewhere else, it's really hot in here, don't you think it's hot in here?"

—Her: "Sure… where do you want to go?"

I don't have an idea in hell where to go; I'm just trying to buy time. Now that's a ridiculous expression, no one can buy time—Bill Gates can't even buy a second of time, we're all gonna die.

I drive her car, since I don't have a car, and let the car decide where to go. In my mind, I practice saying exactly the perfect thing, something out of a romantic comedy, anything so she won't dump me. I build a skeleton out of romance, imagine myself victoriously saying the perfect thing and her swooning. Then I imagine her slapping me and walking the other way. Then I imagine something that I can't quite make out: I'm delivering my pitch, but it's like there's a web over her, a grey/white haze, and I can't see how she'll react I'm lost in my head, everything might happen, whatever does I'm sure already has.

To those unfamiliar with the D.U.I. process: you're able to drive until your hearing.

—

I come to and realize we're at the top of Barker Pass, one of the highest points in Ocean Beach, you can see the islands, you can see everything, the stars, the universe, heaven, and all those in Dante's circles. Now I know why her car took us here—this is where we first were intimate. She's not happy.

She sits up straight, looks at me, moves closer, but stops at an awkward distance. She's closer than an acquaintance, but further than a friend.

—Me: "So what did you want to talk about?"

I'm sweating, she's cold as ice.

—Her: "Why'd you have to choose here?"

All sense of imagined hope for casual geniality is thrown into the wind. Silence. Tension.

—Her: "Sorry, it's just that...."

Her anger has been replaced by vulnerability; maybe this wasn't such a bad idea after all. Tension lowers. More silence, (except a coyote is howling out there somewhere).

After what feels like days:

—Her: "So about last night, I..."

I interrupt. I decide brutally lying to her in the most honest way is the best way to approach this impending disaster—Hurricane Fuck Me.

—Me: "OK, about last night, I'm sorry for being an overbearing, protective asshole. It's just that I care about you, and I saw you with that other guy, and I got jealous. I didn't know what to do, so I drank myself shitty and didn't handle the situation well at all."

My eyes drift to the view, mist starts to settle over the city, and it looks absolutely gorgeous. Better than her even. I look back at her. I don't think my pathetic attempt at a Seth Cohen moment worked, and I try again.

—Me: "Listen, OK, you're the best thing that's ever happened to me. You're smart, (lying), you're interesting, (nose growing), you're beautiful, (true), and you're wonderful, (true at times); any guy would be lucky to have you, (I would). You're everything I could ever hope for, though sometimes I feel less than you. There's just so much I like about you that I pressure myself into not losing you, which leads to me fucking up. After being with you, I just can't imagine not

having you in my life, it would be unbearable.
I…"

Don't say it, don't you dare say it. I need a
fucking drink.

—Me: "I l. o. v. e. y. o. u."

That came out awkwardly; this isn't going
to be good. Hopefully, I talked long enough that
her goldfish attention span dwindled and she's
off thinking about Abercrombie model cock or
something of that genre. She looks bored, like I
just explained to her why, as a military leader, you
should never invade Russia.

I'm fucked.

—Her: "That was really sweet." Yeah, but?
"But last night was just too dramatic. I don't think
I can handle all this right now. I mean I think my
feelings might have changed for you. Just all this
stuff recently has been piling on. I don't know
what to make of it, I'm just not sure I think about
you as a boyfriend, I just don't know if I could see
myself being with you."

You nut-cracking bitch. You… whatever, I
can't believe you just actually said that. I hope
you choke on toothpaste. I hope the condom
breaks when you fuck your Kelly Slater clones,
and his vile scum-sucking AIDS gets in your

pussy rotting your insides; sleep in hell, you gorgeous whore.

—Me: "What." What!

WHAT! SHE JUST THROWS MY HEART OFF THE GODDAMN CLIFF AND ALL I CAN SAY IS WHAT!!!!!

—Her: "I just see us as more of friends."

If you say it's not you, it's me, I will rip your tits off.

—Me: "Listen, all I know is that I feel something different with you than I've ever felt with any girl, when I'm with you, it feels eternal."

I just can't stop from fucking up. My mouth is spewing diarrhea lies.

—Me: "I think it would be a huge mistake to throw something this special away, because of a bad weekend, I need you in my life."

—Her: "Well, I'm really sorry, but I just don't feel like that about you anymore."

It's over. She informs me she has to leave, or she might have said something else, my brain is shut down. She asks for a hug, I just grunt and lean.

She drives away. I sit on the edge of the cliff and watch the sky. I'm not mad, I'm not sad, I feel nothing. It's like the butterflies in my stomach all died at the same time. The nervousness is gone and has been replaced by nothingness. This must be what it feels like to die, minus the vision; maybe if I close my eyes, I'll never wake up. I sit there for hours, I watch the sun rise, and it's the most beautiful moment of my life. Here I am on top of the world, in the lowest pit of self-loathing I've ever known, but I just can't feel sorry for myself. I don't matter, nothing matters.

It matters though, that it's cold. I get up, head home. I don't wish I was dead. I don't wish this didn't happen, I just wish my life was different. I get home. I don't have the faintest idea of what time it is. 8:00? 3:00? Quite frankly, I don't give a damn.

I walk in. I'm loud, but could care less. Nothing matters but it. What the fuck is *it*? If I knew, I don't think it would matter. My mind's clouded. I'm not hungry, I'm nothing, and nothing matters, except *it*, and the fact that I'm crying.

I walk into my room. 9:30. I get into bed with my shoes on, because they don't matter, *it* matters. I close my eyes, and hope for sleep. Thinking to myself about what *it* could possibly be? Is *it* even real, and has it ever been.

RAINBOW
FLAVORED
ECSTASY

Smile too hard and you'll explode. (I think) I've heard this as an expression before, but can't remember. It'd be a funny way to commit suicide; you could do it anywhere. A doctor's office, an elevator, on the toilet. I guess this is why I didn't smile too much when I first met her, at least that's what she said. (God, I hate when people say that). But she liked it. Added mystery to my somewhat bland aura.

We flowed seamless, like liquid in plastic tubes, through life. Fits of passion combusting then eroding over the course of our relationship, slowly permeating our memories making the far, further, and the recent the new memories on which reflection presided. We beat about like boats, toward green lights, blue lights, moths to fire.

Still awake, whole bodies pulsating with the tempo of a new day; explosions in the sky. Suns rising like primordial lava flowing from the earth, or teenage pus from pimples. We lay there, loud but quiet, still but quick. And even though the big hot sun was coming, we could see our breaths touching each other's bodies softly.

Then there was screaming, like we were trying to see our voices, our lungs, and scratching and spitting with crying, creating rivers on which we build boats from what was left, the scraps of happiness. And we would climb in on top of each other to float through life again to something new, something shimmering. Or at least we would pretend it was, until we realized it wasn't, at which point we would just start all over again.

Then, one day, we floated to the beginning of a rainbow. But there was no pot of gold, just a vortex of every color racing to the center of the earth. The colors rising over each other, coursing visible electricity in every direction, trying to get to the bottom of a giant pool of luminous energy, smashing into each other like chemical reactions

creating new shades of electricity, alien concep-
tualizations we'd never seen before—without
even trying we were shaking, rippling, squeezing.
Both of us excited from fear. We had only been
there several moments until a telling whisper
arose from her instinctual curiosity. Her shoulders and legs said she had to know more. Her
fingers released me, she dipped her toe gently
into the screaming vortex of endless color, lights,
and shooting energy. She melted into the vortex
diffusing wildly, dying down into the spinning
chaos, blending to become every color at once, a
part of the plasma, cycling endlessly to nowhere.

At the edge of the pool I had two
choices. I could jump or leave. But I chose to
smile as big and hard as I could, just waiting to see
what happens.

SOPHIE

They sit engaged in the moment, just the three of them—him, her, Sophie. In front of the building everyone goes to during the day; it's not the day; they sit there, just the three of them. Him, her, and Sophie.

They spent their days walking, steps similar, but certainly not the same. They left the dog at home, the one she got for Christmas. And they cried because they'd never seen a child bawl out of pure jubilation.

The next time they saw her cry was next to a malignant x-ray. Then again, when all her stringy little blonde hair fell out. They cried when she was nothing more then a straight fluorescent green line of steady noise and endless stasis.

Now, one year later they sit and sing happy birthday in front of the building where all the people are, but not at night. Their tears fall gracefully mixing with the fog before they kiss the ground: him, her, but no Sophie.

LOVE

I know she loves me. I know she doesn't know she loves me. It's my fault. Something about a night where I walked pigeon toed on my face, my eyes moving in whirlwind frenzies trying to take in the light and sound. Without light sound has no origin. Without light, love has no direction. She is blind. She is deaf. She is a kitten pawing at eternity—eyes blue and white and full of plasma, lost in a love she doesn't know she's fallen into yet.

ALL THE MOLESKINES
IN THE WORLD
AND MINE

1. I see them sitting, writing, thinking all their great original thoughts, on sidewalks, in busses and slouched in chairs. They are our writers, our Fitzgeralds, our Hemmingways, our old dirty men, and the numerous unmentioned who never got to be.

2. They are fucking disgusting. Fragments, arrogant shits that think Celine sank with the Titanic. And they keep fidgeting to keep buds in their ears, smoke cigarettes for the specific reason that they kill. *Spit in the wind: this is our mantra.*

3. There is no three. Three is me, no different from any of those aforementioned caught in the reflective lens of what I assume to be misguided self-hatred. We want to be writers, to be writers so we don't have to write. It is an effortless romantic act, akin to jerking off using a telepathic diaphragm—when you're on ecstasy—RIGHT! That's what Kerouac said with those pop, bam spiders of light. We don't need a stinky fucking message; they'll find it for us. We are the lost and found generation, no responsibility necessary.

13 WAYS FOR
IDENTIFYING A
(SAN FRANCISCO)
HIPSTER

1. At any given moment, in the 7 foggy hills of San Francisco there is a hipster mocking an unwitting pedestrian.

2. There are too many types of hipsters to try and even count, but just like vain attempts at describing pornography: it is known when seen.

3. The hallucination of spokes twirling below a fixie. Hipsters can be found on Valencia feigning cool, it is their wasteland/spawning pool.

4. Boy or girl, both represented. Men and women wearing feathers in their ears are just one. Hipsters are all one.

5. There is only preference in taste, testing the waters to see whose are more original, claiming the underground only to find out your underground is more underground than my underground.

6. Icicle gazes saved for each other, outside the knockout before they empty enough glasses to avow synthetic love. Whilst gulping glasses, look for the squares—a telltale sign of super-imposed taste, worn on the sleeve (which doesn't necessarily constitute clothing) to attract other hipsters that make fun of hipsters who don't think they are hipsters.

7. Oh rejected children of Southern California high schools, wanna be popular? Move to San Francisco with mommy and daddy's money, buy a fedora, a vintage blazer, and discolored t-shirts from the 80's, wear pointy shoes, sunglasses, and an improperly fitting beanie. Always remember never admit to being a hipster.

8. I tried listening to the shitty music that you promised me was good.

I tried reading the nonsensical poets obliterated by obscurity, but then I realized I didn't understand hipster irony, so then I just stopped trying, I guess I'm not smart enough.

9. No hipster, I've never heard of The Tropic Interlopers of Cancer. Should I have? Then they laugh. Laugh me out of the smoking circle. Next time I'll read Pitchfork more thoroughly.

10. Watching them I feel inadequate like there's a handbook I never got. Even the homely poorly tattooed stubby girls seem to understand the hipster hegemony.

11. Then I went down to LA and saw the same people in a different place. Working behind the glass of the same retail stores with the same haircuts. I realized the hipster is universal and ubiquitous.

12. The generations may change, the hipsters will remain, the old become financial consultants with fading tattoos, time capsuled zeitgeist's of irony.

13. It is the rebellion of youth, it is frustration, and it coincides with a monthly parental stipend. The hipster will always live embodied as an over-privileged 20-something.

DIRTY DISHES

An hour late, as usual, and I'm stoned. They'll understand, so long as I make it, (the me being late—not the me being stoned). I throw some water in my hair: dirty with my crazy life, and another weekend without showering. I consider shaving, I decide there's not enough time. Next, I run to Safeway, buy wine, chocolate, shitty dried-out yellow roses—get in my car, shoot south down the 280 to make my obligatory familial appearance.

In my car, making wonderful time for five o'clock on a Sunday, alone, except for all those people in their cars, with their families, friends, and escorts—together, but all by themselves. On my way to see my grandparents, a cousin, and my mom. Thinking of talking points, of positive aspects in my life I can wrap around the obvious negative ones—girls, booze, smoking, etc.—a demonstration in story telling of how I'm becoming an adult (I don't think I'm doing very well in that category).

My mind loses track as I focus on the road. Staring at the yellow lines and trying to avoid the magnetic temptation of cars passing close to me at similar-but-different velocities. I'm extremely stoned, listening to sad Indie music. There's a reason I'm late, maybe not a very good reason, but at least I have a reason—what was it again? They will understand.

My eyes on the road, my mind spinning, drifting to other things, like the girl that my love elevates for, but in futility, with the light skin and pretty hazel eyes that haunt me when I'm still awake against my will at sunrise. Thinking of how bad my kidneys have hurt for the past week. Thinking if I'm even legal to drive with the alcohol I had two hours ago. The pot doesn't count. The music is sad. And she's just as lost as me. If it lasts for a month, maybe I should start worrying. I only had two beers, I'll be fine, I don't remember if the two is factually accurate, maybe because I'm so stoned, I can't swear I didn't have more than two. Maybe I should start worrying that I think the pot doesn't count?

I arrive at Grandma's house a little more than an hour late. I open the door to expected disappointment. Mom standing there with her white hair, piercing blue eyes, and the missing front tooth that she doesn't seem to mind. My grandma, shrunken by age, sitting in a chair, her eyes clouded by cataracts but faintly blue with a gray gloss, sitting, smiling, happy to see me. It's her birthday. My cousin leans on the piano, broad-shouldered from his collegiate-athletic days in the distant past. Middle age is taking over his midsection. The genetics of his eyes are robustly blue, but they lack splendor and curiosity. He's younger than me by a few months, but already has an esteemed nine-to-five, making more money than his parents ever have, stuck with the thought that this might be his forever, crunching numbers in a cubicle doing I'm not sure what. He's been doing it too long for me to appropriately ask what he does. I do know he's got a condo, roommates, a passkey, and a lunch plan. My grandpa, staring at baseball in the downstairs den enjoys a scotch; sometimes when he drinks too much, he shits himself. I can't look him in the eyes (I think they're blue), it's sad, not to mention his crushing emphysema, him huffing away, paying the price for two packs a day x thirty years. Maybe I can't look him in the eyes because I hear him as soon as I arrive; worse: sometimes before I fall asleep, thinking of heredity's guillotine.

After my innate evaluation of the situation I've seen many times over, I rush to Grandma, kiss her, hand her the wine, the chocolates and the shit roses. Also a birthday card. She kisses me, then starts talking shit. In case you don't know, this is a common Irish form of familial expression of affection. I go to say hello to Grandpa. He sits there with his scotch, the TV shining white light on him. Him staring straight ahead. He tries to get up but can't. I lean down, kiss his white, grizzled cheek. I don't dare look him in the eyes.

Upstairs, my cousin leans against the piano, his face twisted in frustration at my tardiness, but he still embraces me. Lastly, my mother, those blue eyes, the first mine ever met. She's happy to see me, she knew I would be late. I follow her into the kitchen and ask if she needs help. "No," she says, but I know she will ask me again in a minute. She tells me I look good, staring into my eyes, eyes of my childhood, green and brown, curious and chaotic. I wish I could say the same to her, but her eyes of irrepressible blue hold a worried stare that has been there for almost two decades. I try to make her happy, and tell her that me and that crazy girlfriend are finally done for good this time [(at least for now) not the hazel-eyed futile love one].

—"Jay, life's hard, and being with someone crazy only makes it harder." Says it with a smile. She's right, but I'm not sure I understand. I know I do, but I also know I never truly will, 'til I find out the hard way. Fucking up is the best way to learn.

I try to smile but I've never been good at forcing a smile. I turn to leave the kitchen.

—"Will you help bring out the food?"

I grab the salad bowl and look for something to protect the table from the steaming, baked chicken in my other hand. She follows me, with bread and potatoes, to a table that is not quite set. My cousin joins us, and my grandma starts her long 10-foot trek from the living room to the dining room. I have to move a chair, the closest to her slowing trajectory. My grandpa('s) remains downstairs, in the static white glow of the TV shining on him. Every now and then, taking a sip of his watered-down scotch—watered-down so he doesn't get too drunk and shit himself.

Grandma, Mom, Cousin and I sit at the table, all of us at different stages of our lives. Bound by blood to spend time together, we sit silenced in awkward tension. No one speaks, and we begin to fill our plates, the chicken steaming in its gray pot in front of my cousin. It doesn't look glorious, but not bad for a beginner senior citizen Irish lady that never learned how to properly cook, (my mom). The salad: overwhelmed with ranch and a disparaging amount of large tomatoes—its saving grace is glorious amounts of avocado topping the leaves, sitting beautifully in a blue bowl. The bread and butter in slices too thick. The mashed potatoes steaming on our plates perched in front of Grandma. Grandpa is still downstairs, the whiskey on the table directly in front of him.

Our plates now filled, my cousin and I begin to pick, my mom and grandma withhold, steadfast in their conviction:

—Mom: "Say grace."

—"No." I say.

—"Why not?"

—"Mom, I will clasp my hands and bow my head, but I will not say grace."

Grandma alleviates the potentially disastrous moment, utters something about the Son, Father, and our daily bread. Then we're allowed to eat.

—Grandma: "So why were you late?"

—"Work meeting—we do this thing every six months where they take us to this brewery and give us a tour, kinda like a welcome for the new employees," says the conductor of my tardiness.

—"Did you drink?" Mom asks, a hint of desperation in her voice.

—"No," I lie.

Of course, I drank, Mom, why do you think I'm late? Why do you think I'm going to leave early? To go drink more.

—"Doesn't anyone else find it ironic that they did this welcome thing in a brewery on a Sunday? I mean, fifty years ago, it would have been in a church."

My buzz interjecting my need to be charming. Mom and Grandma look up from their plates, not pleased. Interestingly, there was a church across the street, but I didn't see anyone there. I cut fast to a safer deluge of conversation, to smother the possibility of my inferred drunkenness.

—"So, Cousin, how you doing? Job goin' well, got yourself a lady?"

— "Job's good, got a few little ladies, nothing too serious."

—"You have a dog yet?"

—"No dog."

—"How's 'bout the social life? Still able get to the bottle?"

Said with the right twist, this can sound like a joke. No dirty looks from my ancestors.

—"I make it work."

This leads to a silence buzzing with anxiety. All of us lost in our cluster of different worries, but for all of us, they feel the same.

—Mom interjects: "Jay broke up with his crazy ex-girlfriend. Again."

—"Good. She wasn't exactly... white." Grandma contributes.

One of Grandma's favorite things to do is exercise her innate ability to separate people based on the pigment of their skin. Sometimes, she's joking, but then again... The world is a different place for me than it is for her, she was in her forties when the civil rights act was signed. She doesn't know you're just supposed to pretend everything's all better, racism is dead, and the civil war is fifth-grade history. Please don't talk about the segregation of San Francisco, there aren't racially divided neighborhoods, just neighborhoods with historical inhabitants. We're not trying to raise rent to drive out the poor. We're not making this street pretty because it will make the rent more expensive. We're not trying to elevate whiteness and oppress the ethnic. That's a conspiracy theory. Why is the truth sometimes a conspiracy theory? My rant, now I'm done with it.

No one says anything, but, "Grandmaaaaa," like we're about to cut to commercial break. Like a little kid just did something on accident.

—Grandma: "I just don't like the idea of you shacking up with a colored girl, and me having brown grandchildren."

I think even if that were to happen, is she naïve enough to believe she'd be around to see them? My family has fun at my expense, berating me about the crazy ex-girlfriend I always hated. And about the alcoholism I use as a joke to cover up the seriousness of the alcoholism. Ever feel like you know where you're going, but you *just **don't care?*** Like you bought a lift ticket that drops your ass off the mountain, into a pit of fire that you're more than comfortable with.

Then the serious questions begin:

—"How's school? What are you gonna do for grad school?"

—"Good, I like my teachers," (not that good, haven't been going to class—hangovers)."I wanna stay where I am," (because that may be the only place I can get into when this bender's over).

—"How's work?"

—"It's, you know, good." (I hate my job more than waking up at eight on a Saturday).

—"How's the roommates?"

—"They're doing fine." (I'm pretty sure we hate each other). These answers offered solely for my mom, to make her feel more comfortable in her academic investment.

My grandpa stumbles to the table. Fortunately, he doesn't smell like shit. He places his drink in front of him at the head of the table. I spot him to make sure he doesn't fall as he sits down.

—"Want some dinner, Dad?" My mother offers.

—"No I'll just have my scotch." This is hardly audible. Before he repeats himself for the third time, desperately trying to be heard, my mom has already cut up some chicken and scooped mashed potatoes. The ridiculously small portion could barely sustain the necessary daily caloric intake of an emaciated nine-year-old. He works on his plate. He looks at me, I look at my plate, empty. His is almost empty. Then I look at him, he's trying with all his focused energy at making the chicken enter his mouth.

After dinner, my cousin makes up excuses and hurries off in haste. I don't know why, but he has work in the morning, and it's the last night he can get drunk for a few days. I'm sure this is on his mind. It would be on mine, and blood is blood. He does the proper goodbyes and races off to the rest of his forever.

Grandpa, now consumed with sloth from his effort at continued existence, is unable to make it back downstairs. He settles for the living room, though it's still ten feet away. Grandma follows him, they turn on the TV, and she holds his hand. The TV light shining on them, separately but equally, blending their vascular fingers. They don't laugh at the TV at appropriate times, which leads me to believe they can't even hear the damn thing. And I already know they can't see it, both have cataracts like a fourteen-year-old mutt. What's the point of hearing and looking at nothing while you're waiting to die? At least they're still together, the TV sharing its white light for both of them.

Mom takes the dishes to the kitchen, the mashed potatoes gone, still a bit of bread, the chicken half gone, the salad almost untouched. Grandpa's empty glass of watered-down whiskey sits near the edge of the table. As Grandpa sits enraptured in nothing, Mom swiftly steals his empty glass of mostly water and a bit of whiskey food coloring. After attempting to talk to my grandparents, then understanding the distance between my mouth and their ears, I walk in the kitchen and ask Mom if she needs help.

—"No," and thanks me for coming to dinner. She says she's proud of me for getting good grades in school, and working hard at the restaurant (read: for not giving up and being the despondent alcoholic that haunts our gene pool). I almost stop her. But can't, so thank her, and feeling a desperate need to escape the room and my consuming shame, tell her I'll ask the grandparents if they want dessert. I do. They say no. Then I walk to the sink and start washing the plates.

They clean up easily except for the chicken. The breading sticks to the bottom of its plate, hanging on desperately, holding, too scared to let go. The bread and butter clean easily, almost not deserving a wash. Potatoes, much the same. The salad requires the disposal.

I ask Mom how to work this thing, she shows me, and I pour the salad in. Along with the salad are the stems of the shitty roses I got my grandma. My mom cuts and waters them. This is unnecessary information, but my mom is a florist. I turn the water on and try to get the plant life to the twisting blades of their fate. There is too much life in the sink. Mom, hearing the disposal struggle, walks over and starts sticking her hand around the edge of the drain. She makes no progress, the garbage disposal still whistling, twisting metal. Frustrated, she dips her hand under the black canvas of protection towards cycling destruction. Upon seeing this, I forget my sedentary high, and belt out, "What the hell are you doing?" grabbing her hand while accidentally pushing her back. She doesn't fall, but I can't remember a time I ever grabbed my mother so forcefully. She doesn't look shocked, just quiet and ashamed. Maybe she remembers doing something similar for me when my head reached no higher than her hip. We walk back to the sink and try to finish the dishes. Everything eventually comes clean. The drying rack fills, and we leave the sink with what formerly held the mashed potatoes, along with two empty glasses of whiskey, two empty vessels (coffins), in the sink of the home my Grandparents have shared for, what to me, is eternity.

Grandma walks in, and asks if we need help, she's always had impeccable timing. We tell her it's fine, it's done. This breaks the silence, the tension, the exchange. I can think of nothing else to do, or say, so I tell them I have homework and should be leaving soon, which means now. Mom is headed back to plastic California (guess which half) in the morning. To her business, to her life, to a home she hopes will one day hold grandchildren. She tries to get me to stay a bit longer. I refuse. I kiss them all goodbye: Grandma and her cloudy eyes; Mom and her penetrating stare. I kiss Grandpa's hair, and wonder if his eyes are still there. If so, what does the world look like? I'm pretty sure his eyes are blue. You could ask my mom, she would know.

I get back in my car, no longer high. As I get on the freeway, I get a text from my lost girl of beautiful color. Promises with lying potential, but in a brief moment of clarity remembering

Newton's third law, I decide not to think with my cock.

I think to myself, I'll drink by myself. Maybe I'll meet new people. The sun has set and with it, my worries of alcoholism. It's not that they aren't there, it's just I don't remember them so easily. I put on some different, sad Indie music. A guy, or boy, or girl, or anyone talking about how life is hard, I still don't think I quite understand. The music still makes me think. I get anxious. Anxious about the pretty girl who says the prettiest things, with light skin, and pretty hazel eyes that I have seen too few times (not Miss Crazy). I can't tell if my kidneys still hurt, which makes me certain that they absolutely do, and I've just gotten used to it. I didn't drink at dinner, never can in front of Mom, I don't want her to see the problem she used to have. And God, I need some fucking pot.

I get closer to home, the anxiety plateaus, always there but not as extreme when I am in motion. I look out at the white lights, not of the city, but the suburbs. I look at the houses on hills where there was once grass and think of how many people each light represents. If you have more lights to represent you, does that make you more important? I think about the white light on my grandparents' faces from the TV they weren't even watching. The two of them holding hands, barely living, still touching, still here. Maybe that's the way to go? Sitting and touching.

Then, I remember, the fear and worrying tonight will be the last time I ever see them. I wonder if they're thinking the same thing. I hope they weren't. If they weren't, it makes me happy to know that there is a quiet kindness in death.

GETTING FUCKED ON AN EMPTY STOMACH

It's not gonna be a riot. There isn't that other-world tension: thick as fog, chewy as taffy. It feels more like a pep rally.

And then we pile in, we're cattle, and take the train to where our cause will die.

I stare at Fitzgerald and eavesdrop. The tram is compacted; the tram is fractured.

I see hazy eyes, smell cheap booze. All I can think to myself is "just another excuse to get wasted." The guys are wearing stretched out tank tops to expose their puberty gifts, and the girls write dull messages on their boobs. I saw the word slut written a lot, apparently it rhymes with cut?

We arrive like a fart, wafting all about, taking escalators and singing maligned chants, going no-where, but always walking. I find a familiar face, smoke a bowl, and feel the time is right to leave. All around, fragments, circles, marching nowhere fast to nothing, lacking inter-connectivity in this chaos, all those feet marching to the crack of what might as well be a banshee yelling on a megaphone about something or other. Of this I am certain. The little kids are marching too, but they have no idea why.

I have no idea what this all is: it's a field trip, an excuse to miss class.

I'm already lost, but for them, the too young, why destroy their innocence? We're using them.

Fuck it. I walk 5 blocks to a dive, trying to get a beer. I enter and smell a burning cigarette. The barmaid/man, I can't really tell, pays very little attention to me. I ask her for something foamy, she/he neglects me while working his/her way up some fat construction worker's leg for a good tip. I understand.

The beer sweats, the bubbles flying to the surface, compressing, nothing, only for another bubble to follow. Bubble after bubble, always more bubbles achieving nothing, going nowhere, popping without ever knowing it happened.

I drink a few more beers, have some personal time with F. Scott, and move on. Walking south past the demonstration, the rally, the apocalypse... the fart. I see fewer police officers than I did outside high school keggers.

It all feels so pacified, so planned, so *quarantined*. The government does not give a shit. They want us to be unhappy. And when we're unhappy they want us to protest, so they can pretend that we've made a difference, and we pretend we've done all we could. Those with true sway are 20 years removed from their education, from passion, too busy making sure their children (and in return themselves) will not be fisted by the slow agony of drowning debt. Those with true sway are insuring that the peaceful protest turns into a field trip. They relax with their medications, swirling brown liquor in glasses with no stems—pure crystal—knowing we suffer; and when we suffer, sometimes we turn to crystal. Why couldn't they, at the very least, make squatting (or drugs) legal?

The government couldn't be happier. They know we're rallying and they're pleased. They're

practically fucking begging us to. In all this pas-
sive activism, a practice in vanity, just being able
to tell your friends you were there is enough.
These March 4TH whispers have been screamed
for months. Why March 4TH? Couldn't we have
at least had some historical perspective, something
meaningful like perhaps the 15TH—of course the
budget cuts affect education.

And this makes us feel good about ourselves,
builds our confidence, like a parent's compliment
to a child's hapless artwork. So we sleep, home,
happy, and tired, with the sweat of almost revolution, refreshed by our designer couture: imagine a
lilac body-wash. But it's still the same. We're getting fucked in every hole, too much oral fixa-
tion to eat, so we're starving and screaming and
sleeping in the streets, begging, pleading, trying
so hard to revolt in the most genial of matters.
But a revolution it is not, just ask Fanon.

THE NEW OPIATE
OF THE MASSES,
BUT NOT CRYSTAL METH
({OUR} LOVE IS DEAD)

Love is dead, like god before her. Banished to the back rooms for the plebeians to cut their teeth on.

The Sophists are crying, the teenagers are every bit as confused. The stoics go to work anyway; for them, nothing's happened.

This isn't coming from overwhelming heartbreak, or familial rejection, it's just the synthesis of realizing innocence crossed our eyes, dotted our Tee's, then made us blind and believe anything possible. But hope is a four-letter word.

It's coming from triple scoop days with extra gummy bears of plasma green, realizing that sometimes when your daddy didn't come home at night it's because he was working late, but not to support mommy. Then realizing your dad has a dick just like yours. And that this sex thing went from being this scary Pandora's Box themed roller coaster of intrigue to the reference point for absolutely everything and anything in your life. Then you had it and it sucked and you rolled up on the bed next to your lover, reeking of the wrong brand of cigarette. Sweat and improperly cleaned orifices. Just lying there, not crying, holding your junk, embarrassed and shame filled, pleading with the dark. And with closed eyes to no one, you want an explanation, desperately wishing you could ask your mom, "What's going on?"

But Marvin Gaye's dead, and the Disney movies have changed. Prince Charming is a drunk, Cleopatra a whore, and your parents might have gotten married based on conception, proximity, or fear of being alone. Maybe they were happy, but are they now? Being in love is being alone with somebody else who could never understand how you feel. But you think they do because you're speaking the same language and the words are so beautifully curved in similarity. Language is a compromise, and we can never actually touch.

Only get so close we trick our senses into thinking it's real: who can trust the senses anyway? As
Renee would say, the only thing that is, is your
"I" (eyes?). So maybe sometimes I'll fall, I'll trip,
I'll stumble, but love is dead so let's kill pretending with it. Get this over with, we're just going to
be shit miserable and hate each other in the end.
So good-bye love, I renounce you and please do
kindly and flounder the fuck off.

TWO FRIDAYS

Baseball players' eyes smile with french-fried filled mouths and a memory in the making makes me forget the gold-toothed elderly Yiddish gypsy with boils who cursed me over her breath drowning out my attempted apology at near obstruction.

In the eyes of reflection there's symbolism in everyone's appearance: save for those we are close to—too close to see the obvious and the faults only because without these obvious faults, they would never be the torch of generations, whose time we happen to share. The wick slowly burning, we call them "friends," "brothers"—for a lucky few, both.

We're already soil, which for me raises the question: is it better to be a pile in a box, or the felt on fingertips transposed through the roots of trees?

Kiss eyelids while you can, because blinking is a privilege every man one day loses to an eternal glare of self reflection. That, and a longing for the ability to go back and make all the same little mistakes.

There's freedom in a cigarette, in death. It's a slight grasp on the handle of nothingness, which, once opened, leaves the soul empty. Choices are nothing; it's the ability to choose that's important.

So choose LIFE! Choose death and fresh pineapples, but most importantly choose to kiss your mother on the cheek after she's had a bad day.

LINES,
WALL STREET,
AND PUPPIES

Lines, lines, all these lines rule and dictate all our lives.

Lines at the movies, at registration, lines on the coffee table.

Apparently we're too stupid for our own good. If the inventor of the line had copyrighted it, he would be rich. By default he'd be the ultimate and supreme chancellor of Earth. Bill Gates would suck the sweat from his balls for nickels.

The bureaucracy is comforting, like a big stupid puppy that shits everywhere, it's pretty to look at, but flawed, clumsy, and overall just a huge fucking mess (me?). And it should be euthanized (the bureaucracy, not the puppy—unless the puppy bites like nature itches him to), but what would you replace it with?

So: lines on your face, your fruit, your fucking heart, your brains, your feet, lines in the sand! All we are are lines, and questions of how to get in them.

THE DARK NIGHT STILL LEADS TO MORNING

They found him lying there—dead. The discoverers didn't know he had been shot in the head, and once the destruction had become clear they could literally see his mind. Where there was once a universe of ideas and desires, there was now a void splash of oozing mush, the colors running, making their original distinction impossible to determine.

The two young men, Charlie and Jay, both twilight teenagers from comfortable backgrounds, were stumbling between alleyways en route to their parentally funded bachelor condo; the nuzzling crest of the sun just peeking his nose over the edge of the sky to look where he must travel today. The two "men" were brazenly recounting conversations that happened barely two hours ago when they came across Mathias. The light in its transitory state did not do justice to the seriousness of Mathias' brain splattered mess. At first they took him to be an active member of the booming transient movement.

Common sense is something all young people think they have, but these young drunkards had none. This is why when their parents were chatting with their friends they would lie and say their kids had it all together. But not so secretly, and often silently in the depths of their minds, every six or seven heartbeats, they worried about their children's futures (and then their own). Charlie's and Jay's minds thought mostly of carnal realization six of every seven seconds, and on the seventh they rested and thought of nothing at all.

—Jay (to the dead man): "Hey buddy."

Jay tried instigating interaction, in turn provoking Charlie—the moon and the sun doing their dance, the city's horizon gently starting to glow.

—Charlie screeched: "Yo Scumbucket!"

Then turning to Jay out of the side of his mouth:

—Charlie: "This motherfucker must be more hammered than me. Should we wake him up?"

—Jay: "Dude are you kidding me? This dude hasn't showered since he lost his house. Let's leave him alone, let him get some sleep."

—Charlie: "No dude! Let's call the cops and get him arrested. Come on dude it will be hilarious. It's not our fault this piece of shit wasn't smart enough to avoid liquidation."

—Jay: "Char, you gotta remember sometimes it's not so simple. Sometimes shit happens,"

—Charlie: "Shit happens for a reason. You really need to read Ayn Rand, she explains this all very eloquently, and there's sex, what more could you ask for."

—Jay: "Yeah, I'm gonna take Lit. advice from a business major. That meritocratic bullshit is like catnip for you. For fuck's sake Char, you cite *Unbearable Lightness* as your justification for banging hookers in Peru, while spending the same amount of money that could have inoculated an entire African country."

—Charlie: "Yeah that may be true… total-ly worth it. Took some Viagra, got my money's worth, and I was the fucking man."

Jay, with unrestrained laughter, his face form-ing a hard 'V,' threw his hand to his mouth and undulated naturally, air barely making its way through his teeth, the sun winning its coup with the moon, slowly crawling its path to where it started, where it will continually circle until it gets tired, exploding and then we'll all sleep—forever.

—Charlie: "Come on Jay, you know you want to go to South America and bang some fine hookers with big fake titties."

Jay laughed, managing to huff out:

—"I'll pass."

As the last 's' left his mouth, it pulled with it a fresh streak of vomit, food he just paid for with his dad's credit card. His eyes became consumed with an "I think I'm gonna die" look. Then he lost his footing, and unconsciously falling next to his future, void of consciousness.

—Charlie: "What the fuck, man, are you ok?"

Charlie was now staring at the pile of death directly in front of him. Staring hard into the man's absence of spirit, and then when he felt he had ascertained all he could from the image, he blinked and looked away. Before he called the cops, he dialed one last possibility of vital release, his favorite sperm depository, a way to end the night. She didn't answer. Half irritated Charlie gave up on the night and dialed the obligatory 3 numbers in case of emergency, or if you need a grown up.

Jay gained consciousness shortly after Charlie, on his cell, explained the situation to the police.

—Jay: "Let's get out of here."

—Charlie: "No, we gotta wait for the cops."

Jay called his parents, asked them what to do, they couldn't give him an answer, so he hung up. They waited for the police, consumed with death while the sun continued smiling brighter and bigger.

The next day Charlie called Jay and asked him to go to a bar. Jay said no.

—Charlie: "Lots of fine bitches."

Jay hung up the phone.

The obituary was never printed, only the autopsy report, in part because there was no family member to write it or confirm the man's identity. In full because the man made headlines as the autopsy revealed he was at least 150 years old.

—TV Reporter: "A man of undeterminable ethnicity was found this morning in an alleyway by two young students near the university."

—Charlie: "It was dark, at first we thought he was sleeping, then it was bright enough, and we could see it—him—more clearly."

—TV Reporter: "The police reportedly said the young men were intoxicated: however, they are not under suspicion with regards to the man's murder. Two neighborhood bartenders confirmed the young men's alibis at the precise time the coroner believes the victim was fatally shot in the head. The autopsy also revealed that the old man appeared in perfect health. "

—Coroner: "Considering the condition his heart, lungs, etc. there is no way to accurately gauge how much longer he would have lived, but definitely longer than his 150 years. It's quite fascinating."

—TV Reporter: "One of the young men refused to identify himself and said in a state of shock:

—(Jay):'He looked old, you know, like grandparent old, but like, not *that* old.'"

—TV Reporter: "When asked how he felt about discovering the corpse of the oldest reported living human in modern history, the young man replied:

—(Jay): "'No comment.'"

—TV Reporter: "The dead old, old, old man may not be remembered since no one has come forward to identify the body. Speculation would suggest everyone he'd known over his lifetime has long since passed; sad beauty in a sad life. But the dead man did have a DMV ID card in his pocket, identifying him only as Mathias Adam. His corpse was taken to UCSF for extensive re-search to understand the bodily abnormalities that allowed him to achieve such great age."

The phone rang.

—Jay's Dad: "You were on CNN, did you see it?"

—Jay: "Dad, I don't want to talk about it."

Jay hung up. He then got up, paced around, then sat back down. He couldn't think of any-thing other than how loud everything sounded when you're all by yourself.

A month later Charlie called.

—Charlie: "Dude stop being a bitch, kick it with me, we'll do something to take your mind off of being an emo-kid and then we'll get shit-faced."

—Jay: "No, I don't feel like it man."

—Charlie: "Look, I'm coming over and we're going to get loose, and you're going to fuckin' like it, or I am gonna go over there while you're sleeping and tea bag the shit out of you. Plus I think this will help you decompress, let the air back in."

—Jay: "If I say no, are you going to come over anyway?"

—Charlie: "Already on my way."

Charlie's black beamer pulled up to Jay's dorm. Jay got in.

—Charlie: "How's dorm life Jay, banging lots of ladies in the shoebox you share with that creepy Asian kid?"

—Jay: "It's fine, easier for me to study here."

—Charlie: "Should have never moved out. It's been a wild semester. Where the fuck have you been? We haven't raged together in like a month. You just been reading depressing books about sad boys in love?"

—Jay: "Nope."

—Charlie: "What then?"

—Jay: "Whitman, Stevens, Sartre… Joyce."

—Charlie: By choice?

—Jay: "Yep."

—Charlie: 'Well, what have you been doing for fun?"

—Jay: "Nothing."

They sat in silence as the black car flew onward toward death, toward twilight, lost in paradise.

—Charlie: "Get out."

—Jay: "Where are we?"

—Charlie: "You'll see."

They pulled up to the door of a large cement building with purple neon sign crafted to represent a handgun, in a neighborhood full of trucks. Jay looked on ambivalently as Charlie opened the door.

Standing there wearing earmuffs, glasses, holding a tiny black piece of metal, they could hear nothing over the cracks of death intended, so nothing was spoken. Charlie put the picture of Osama on the line, pushed a button, and so back he flew. Charlie fired eight shots, pressed the button, back came the sheet of paper. Charlie pointed excitedly, then gestured to Jay as to say with his body: your turn. Jay tried to refuse; pointing to his eyes, claiming with his hand he wouldn't be able to see, having forgotten his glasses. But with guile, his learned wit with pantomime (all part of being a business major), Charlie convinced Jay without the medium of words.

Jay stood facing the figure eye to eye. He breathed short and heavy, his hand shaking as if it were the morning after that night. He looked at the paper. The face had changed. It was the old man, Mathias. The lifeless stare gazing no-where, contributing nothing, his energy returned to the world, nothing. Then the face warped. It was Jay's face, his eyes staring into nowhere. He had become the old man. Out of instinctual fear, Jay fired, and fired again, then again, and... now empty clicks. The gun dropped with his hand. Jay felt nothing. He was the old man. Jay pressed the target button, but hardly looked at the target. Charlie tried to pretend to feign interest.

As they left the building, Charlie suggested a BBQ place several blocks away. Jay suggested they walk. Charlie found that agreeable. As they walked, Charlie tried to talk; Jay tried to respond, but nothing clicked. And so on they walked. As they were passing a fruit stand, colored more beautifully than lights at your first rave, Jay came to a dead stop in front of shiny yellow Asian pears. They looked particularly good, accented by the heat of the day in a record breaking January.

—Jay: "Charlie grab me a pear."

—Charlie: "What?"

—Jay: "Just do it, grab me a pear."

Charlie inspected the fruit stand and realized there was no attendant. Maybe he was bangin' a mistress, maybe he was burning in protest. Charlie grabbed the pear and tried to hand it to Jay. Jay refused.

—Jay: "Take a bite, then give it to me."

—Charlie: "Why?"

—Jay: Char, my friend, please."

—Charlie: "Okay Jacob, but you're weird."

Charlie bit it and Jay grabbed the fruit, looked at it momentarily, nervous, his eyes consumed. Then he plunged into his first bite. He continued to devour the fruit and started to walk. Charlie followed, confused and hungry. The sun hung in the same place it would have the day of their shared discovery of death (maybe a little bit higher).

—Charlie: "Why did we do that?"

—Jay: "Don't worry about it. Let's go eat."

They walked into a restaurant, shooting the shit, talking about somethings that are nothing to anyone else. Charlie looked at the ladies, Jay did

too—no longer consumed with death—thinking: all floating bells must come down.

BARELY ENOUGH

All the windows with their big lights and little people. The eyes for the dense-cloud night.

The ground shakes, but it's not the "big one," just the train.

—"So can I kill it?"

—"Go for it."

I try hiding my disappointment, but there's no way; it's as thick in my voice as the water in air scattered through the night.

He doesn't say anything, polishes off the bottle, twists a grimace, and gives a post shot exhale. The bottle smashes to the ground.

—"How much cash you have?"

—"Three, four bucks."

—"Fuck."

Half thoughts ensue and then a light, for ciga-rettes. The moods still finding itself, and there's no foreshadowing about the state of the imposed night. It's not one of those times, where the universal line drags you along, a spectator of your own fate.

—"What about you?"

Blank look.

—"How much cash, you stupid fuck?"

Filled look.

—"Maybe 4 bucks and some change."

—"Looks like were gonna have to settle for plastic."

I go into the market across the street, and buy some vodka with a long, supposedly Russian name. I ask for matches, get them, leave, twist the cap and take a pull.

—"How much does that leave us with?"

—"Looks like we're begging the bus driver tonight."

We kill the bottle.

GREEN LIGHT

Green light. That's the last thing she said. She said it the last time I saw her, and right before she left. I remember the green shawl that made her eyes explode like neon fireworks dancing brilliantly around the rings of her irises. I remember when I had the pleasurable but unfortunate experience of making direct eye contact. Her gaze was powerful enough to consume us both. But I didn't dare breakaway 'cause then she would have to, all the while my back screaming, crawling like crickets, nails, and crabs.

Brown is the color of shit. Her hair was not brown. It fell past her shoulders and not a hair out of place; shining, illuminated like a polished table under the dining room chandelier, even on cloudy days. And those blonde runners, not so much blonde but gold, accenting the chocolate fuchsia that looked better than in the magazines. Her hair surrounded the circles on her cheeks, tiny freckle cherry-blossoms blooming when she blushed. Her smile was the jewel in the middle, radiating light like a diamond as big as the Ritz.

But then she didn't laugh as much. And for no reason at all we began to disagree. I never built up the proper courage to kiss her at the right times. Times when she was insecure, and sad, and felt like shit. I could have grabbed her and promised things would be okay, even if they weren't, and I'd say I'd push harder than Sisyphus, shoulder to rock, straight into to the sun, until either the boulder melted, or I did.

I never did though. Then silences grew un-comfortable and more uncomfortable because of how uncomfortable the previous silenc-es had been. The silences, crazy conversations unto themselves with words running chaotical-ly unsaid. We started to fuck less, and we would both make excuses not to when the subject arose. Times she previously would have laughed became altercations.

I'm not trying to say it was all her fault, it wasn't, it's just the mere form of her didn't help. Like I could do nothing but fuck up, everything I'd say was a fuck up, everything I did another fuck up, and the situation became one, something based on nothing, where the quiet was silence, and that's all that it was.

Then one day we got in the car, and she said something; it was quiet, the words didn't matter. A tear fell down her cheek, and she almost laughed. Then she started talking faster, and faster, and faster. Then she stopped with the car. A mother walked by, her child on her shoulder. She dropped her keys. When she reached down to pick them up, her daughter extended her hands and grabbed the keys, handed them to her mother and laughed unhindered—it was something beautiful, a passing moment. Our eyes caught, painfully, something beautiful, a passing moment. And I broke, my eyes. The ligaments of our connection tearing slowly away. Then the light changed, I couldn't move my foot, maybe I just didn't want too, with no words formulating in my arena of sentience. She said:

—"Green light."

4:30

Bars close at 2 a.m. in California, a nuisance for the dedicated alcoholic. Stumbling, fumbling words, spirit, and memory—creating lost connections that evaporate into the cosmos, leaving energy that might not have existed at all. And your friends smile when you see them at 4:15—15 minutes before your shift—loosely lubricated in bourbon's brown, oily haze that stoked this hazy fire of next day halfie's, not drunk but not entirely sober. Sometimes I'm charming; a friend says you bought a rose for a beautiful Cuban girl you fell in love with outside of Vertigo. You said some charming things in broken Spanish, she smiled. You kissed her cheek—prompting a giggle—and then she furtively slipped away, encased in a protective box created by her unfortunate looking friends. But, you made her smile.

—They were just jealous, because they wanted it too.

My friend laughs.

Then there are the nights when you don't sleep 'til halfway through brunch, and your alarm goes off, your throat burning like the Gobi. But getting up hurts too much. You roll over.

You catch the last alarm, the one that if you missed, it would result in a week without getting paid, sitting at home emptying bottles. But luckily, like always (somehow) shit connects and you beat about, not like boats, but like the wings of a hummingbird spastically flying about the ruins of what could be a nice apartment, collecting the necessities. Throw the shirt you've worn for the last three days into the drier, vanishing the wrinkles and musking the pot flavored B.O. you seem to have developed. No time to shower, dry shave, it hurts, but life's tough, sometimes a helmet is necessary. You pray the bus is waiting at your door.

4:30 again. Same friends you saw 12 hours ago, saying nothing. This time the executor of my drunken state doesn't come up to me and smile. I attempt banter:

—"Motherfucker, last night was crazy."

Considering the vacancy of memory, this is normally a safe thing to say. But this time my forced charm isn't met with reciprocity, but with a burdened stare, a broken voice and strange tears. Nothing can be understood in the hectic attempts to elucidate the dead night. My drinking buddy sounds like Bob Dylan, but from Scotland, after losing his first dog:

—"Tony... North Beach... pizza... fight... head... pavement..."

Pause, then tears turn his eyelashes into icicles:

—"Tony punched this dude... and one of the guy's friends came up behind him, hit him with a bottle, and he smacked his head against the pavement."

No more. I feel my pupils shrink like raisins and can't look my buddy in the eye. I can't cry, tears are pointless and sometimes it's better (easier) to avoid being human.

Why is it you always promise to quit drinking on Mondays, when everything bad happens on Saturday, sometimes on Tuesday. I've heard rumors of Wednesday having wildly unfortunate happenings, but rarely travesties. Good Fridays are great because of *g*od, and Sundays are serene unless you happen to work at this restaurant.

I hated Thursdays when I was in grade school,
I think because of lunch, but college repaired
my relationship with Thursday. Something about
Saturdays always seems to suck. And on Sunday
I drink again, because the shift was hard, San
Francisco's cold, and Tony's in a coma.

STARING THROUGH THE HAZE

1. THE ORDER OF ADDICTION

Another day (depending on which) leads to the exchange of x amount of dollars, seeking refuge in liquid glass (or plastic)—and the happiness promoting power of granulated white sands, depending on the bronchioles, the day, and contents of your wallet (and of course *time*).

You enter the world, buy a coffee, or don't if you're low. No matter what you'll just make it. Two dollars saved, better wasted on eight cigarettes.

When you get back, or if you didn't leave (made the coffee), smoke, drink the coffee and given the economics of time, you shower, or you don't, depending when you brought yourself back to the world, possibly dry shave, go to work.

At work your mind runs only from table to table. Sometimes you're still drunk.

2. THESE ARE THE BEST DAYS

Then the clock clicks, you're exhausted. You float to your version of "Cheers," try and get drunk enough to feel it in the morning.

Sometimes you have the day off, these are the worst. What are we to do when we don't have someone to tell us? I guess that's why you call your girl, and she arrives in a black Mercedes. Somehow it's always Thursday, maybe those are my days off. You pay $50 dollars for the drip of confidence.

Nights are spent on barstools, rooms of friends, or the basement of a club where the wobbles are free on Thursday.

You end up cabbing home, alone, mind shaking with anxious paranoia. It's always Thursday—with thoughts of this and that. This. That. THIS. THAT. This that. Then that before this.

You tell him to drop you off 5 blocks from your house, maybe the morning light will clear your clearly cluttered brain.

3. STARING THROUGH THE HAZE

Staggered footsteps, puke on corduroys, and a hangover capable of bending time.

Still lit neon signs, steam seeps up into the street over sand into coffee cups. Cars move at a tired velocity towards a contrived society.

No wallet, no phone, no keys. Lost somewhere in the gaps of the still fading night.

I feel light.

Depressed corner lots, destroyed windows, malfunctioning signs. I take an unexpected stumble into the middle of the street, get scared for no reason—no cars in sight, either direction.

Hurt, I look up, the orange and purple blends into what I take to be the tops of my eyes. The situation would be unbearable without the now dwindling chemical assistance of the previous/current night.

Staring through the haze, it's almost beautiful.

LOVE AND MUSIC

Music doesn't have to exist, but it does. Love doesn't have to exist, but it might. One of the most beautiful variables of the human capacity is the universally innate understanding and appreciation for the beauty that enriches the human experience—that jubilant realm of the intangible, the inexplicable, its only certainty that it makes life more enjoyable. That's why the "artist" (an umbrella term) is so celebrated. His/her duty is to capture the unexplainable, ubiquitous beauty that defines our mortal procession. Sometimes even the artist doesn't understand the impact of his/her work, but can feel the weight, the beauty of humanity pressing against his/her brain's fingertips.

GIRLS - CAROLINA

I wanna pick you up, Baby,
throw you over my shoulder
Take you away, I wanna carry you home.

We're sitting in her room. We both just got off work. We're there, chain-smoking, snorting lines, and drinking Irish whiskey. Sometimes, when we don't feel like going out (rarely), we just sit in a room, and drink, and talk while listening to music: those are my favorite nights with her. We make a playlist, mix a drink, snort a line, light a ciggy.

—"I've been trying to write about you lately, but nothing will come. There are times that I desperately want to drop everything I'm doing and turn you into poetry. A beautifully unrealistic, Picasso cat lady made of words. That inspiration mainly comes at inopportune times, however, like when I'm driving. Then when I get home, I sit down to get out all my pretty thoughts about you. The abstractions become fog and all that drips from my fingertips is clouded prose. I think it's because I haven't been reading."

I decide to start her with a doozy, it's already one in the morning, and I'm too tired for formalities.

—"You absolutely need to start reading again. Look at you, you stopped writing, and you've lost words in conversation three times this week. You used to roll your eyes searching for the word and, within seconds, your lips would follow with pure beauty."

Her voice holds a degree of seriousness I brought on myself:

—"You're letting yourself go to shit, becoming a premature stereotype."

Normally, if she'd hit me with this line, I would just smirk, smile, make her giggle, pin her down, and hold her shoulders, breathing slowly at first but steadily faster, the whole time trying to spin the conversation away from the numerous substance abuse problems I definitely have. Knowing the whole time she is more than entirely right. Then we lie next to each other like Siamese twins, half connected, half in our separate thoughts, fixated on the other. I start to smile in response, but before I can charm her into forgetting what she just said, she starts with the same matter of fact seriousness:

—"You're leading yourself down this path of self-destruction and substance abuse. It's okay to waste time, but you're wasting too much time. And the way you're wasting time is greatly reducing your life expectancy."

TRACK 2. BARNACLE GOOSE - BORN RUFFIANS

And I'm frustrated with myself,
but I can't change
Don't want to be me anymore.
With all these ticks and tocks and
clicks of clocks that tell timeeee
Tell me this is just a phase.

Slightly taken back, I start to defend myself against her truth. To seem more convincing, I look her in the eye:

—"Sometimes fiction can demonstrate life better than life can explain fiction. To create fiction, you have to understand life, or at least your version of it. For me to do this, I need to remove myself from seeing things with a neat construction of the fiction I want to create. To be able to properly construct fiction, you need to see the mess of life's certain capriciousness."

My voice starts rising with what you could mistake for confidence in what I'm about to say, my inflection almost convincing myself that I know what I'm talking about:

—"With all life's confusing victories, haunting heartbreaks, and nights full of vibrant conversation and multi-liquored cocktails, it's hard not to feel like Gatsby. To remain a protagonist in my nonfiction, I disengage from pen and page to live and experience life. Hopefully, three months from now, I'll be writing beautifully ironic prose with witty allusions about the three months that preceded the writing."

I look away from her eyes. Her magical, mercurial eyes. Staring at me like God or Eckelberg. You'd have to ask her which one she believes in. I look to the green candle burning next to the MP3 player. The candle sits on a collection of prose/poetry I wrote to impress her. The same collection got into the hands of medium-sized publisher who got hard over it. Then, without process or thought I start again:

—"There is a danger though. There's always the possibility that three months from now, I'll be doing the same shit I am now. Drinking shitty liquor that punches you in the liver like a prize-fighter. Snorting various white powders 'cause the bottle isn't enough. Smoking too many cigarettes, pot, cigarettes dipped in cocaine. Still not shooting, but getting high day-in, day-out. Letting the luster of an idea fade, becoming one of those dreams differed. 'Til one day my nose is too clogged to get the powder in my blood-stream, so I get a spoon, a string, and a prick. If that happens, I'm gone. It's happened to friends, they've become the walking dead, their dreams imploded, lying flat on the floor of their swiftly fleeing souls."

TRACK 3. **STRANGE VINE - DELTA SPIRIT**

It's such a strange vine
wrapped around my neck bone
The sun came while you were shining
The tide flew when we were
writing a symphony in the key of D
Songs that had lost their luster
finally they found their color.

—"But that's terrible. You're actively seeking self-destruction. You don't have to be a fuck-up to be a writer. You always say that stupid Hemingway quote: 'Write drunk: edit sober.' Well, take some of your own goddamned advice. You've been consistently intoxicated or inebriated for nearly four months, destroying yourself with a smile. Giving death the finger six feet from his own door. Yes, you're right. F. Scott, Kerouac, Bukowski were all raging alcoholics, but they didn't have a penchant for powder, or that lazy grass you're always on. Plus, Kerouac and Fitzgerald died tragically young. Bukowski should have died tragically young but was saved by some deranged woman that took his shit. You don't have to try and be them to be a writer, be original. You're better than this."

Her tonality shifts from intense to inquisitive:

—"Think about it. When was the last time you went a day stone-cold sober? When was the last time you were so tired, you could barely hold yourself, sober, sleeping all through the night? Not this chemical-induced confusion you avow to need to sleep properly. For fuck's sake, Jay, look at the bags under your eyes, big as a baby's fists. Most importantly, when was the last time you put more than three goddamned sentences on the page consecutively?"

Again, I know she's right, but I try not to show it, and I see she can see that I know she's right. Then, again without thinking about what I'm saying, I start:

—"Maybe this time I can't stop! Maybe I've passed the tipping point!"

I say this as flatly as a human can in regards to their accelerating mortality. She looks straight at me so hard, I can see myself in her eyes.

—"Aren't you afraid you'll die young?!"

She pauses, reconstructs the question she intended to be rhetorical into an inquisition of genuine curiosity:

—"Do you think you'll die young?"

She says this staring straight at me, her eyes doughy as usual but wide and more alert than normal. She refuses to blink.

—"I... I... I've thought about it before. I just... I don't know."

I pull my eyes away with the last word. She open-palm slaps me as hard as she can. This makes me momentarily cross-eyed with cuckoos spinning 'round my head. I understand her intent, after several seconds of mental recomposition.

My eyes heavy as boulders. I pull them off the floor back to her eyes ablaze with blue fire.

—"What the fuck, Jay! How can you talk like that? At the very least, lie to yourself like you do about everything else. Lie to yourself for me, Jay. What about me? What would I do if one morning you didn't wake up before me like you always do? So I decide to let you sleep and walk to the kitchen to make us coffee, light our morning cigarettes. I come back into our room to wake you. My morning lulls receded; I realize you're not breathing."

She's speaking steady as a metronome with circumscribed determination. Hiding behind the veil of determination, a remote quiver, her playing out the scenario in her mind's eye.

—"What if we had kids, Jay? What if they found you face-down in a pile of your own piss? Me in the kitchen too busy with sliced apples, sack lunches, making granola with yogurt, my mind wondering when the fuck you're going to get up, and give me a hand! What about that?"

She punctuates in a way that allows me to infer it's my turn.

TRACK 4. **SOMEDAY SOON - HARLEM**

Someday soon, you'll be on fire
And you'll ask me for a glass of water
I say no...You can just let that shit burn
And you'll say, Please, please, please put me out
I promise not to do it again
Whatever I did to you.

Again, without the advantage of knowing what
the fuck I am about to say, I begin:

—"You don't know what it's like to be in
my head. When the winds blow at the cooling
twilight, I'm all by myself. Sometimes it's about
death, or lack of life, or the horrors of Darfur,
the homeless of L.A., all that esoteric humani-
tarian shit that is always around. Mostly though,
it's about *you*. You running around with all those
pretty things you call friends. It's nights like these
you won't answer your phone or so much as
burp in my direction. It comes from you being so
damn indecisive. You can't figure out if you're in
love with me, or if you just love the pretty words
I paint you with. If that's the case, then you're in
love with yourself. What about you, Daisy? What
are we doing right now, all the same fucked-up

shit we normally do? And I can write when I'm doing this shit!"

I stop and slow down. I look up at her and talk as softly as I can, trying to remember what it's like when she refuses to sit in the same room as me.

—"The only time I can't write is when you're messing me around. You know you're playing the actress in the title role of a movie called 'Jay's Self-Destruction.' You wanna know why I haven't written a word in three months? Because I've been with you… I've been trying to appreciate you being in my life before you blow away like Remedios, a flower landing on different hipster boys' shoulders, melting their hearts like butter. Laughing with your head on their shoulder, or in their lap, then crying in the street a week later, because your puppy love died. Then you crawl into my bed, because you hate sleeping alone, and me all fucked-up because I'm afraid of losing you."

TRACK 5. **OUR DEAL - BEST COAST**

I wish I could tell you how I really feeeel
I wish I could tell you, but that's not our deal.

—"There's nothing more that I'd like to do
than lay in bed all day getting stoned, watching
movies, playing our favorite songs for each other.
Then we would go out and eat breakfast, drink
mimosas, and waste lazy Sundays on the patios
of our favorite bars. But you're a fucking flapper
that time-traveled from the 'teens to wreak havoc
on boys prone to broken hearts. You're a fucking
muse confused out of your pretty little head. You
just want to experience everything at once and
separate. You couldn't make up your mind if you
were held at gunpoint.
    I take a breath.
    —"But I would *never* change anything, be-
cause then you wouldn't be the beautiful mess
that you are. I love your ethereal curiosity and
your ode against boredom. I love watching you
love life, your eyes full of shiny gold flakes. I love
when I wake up half drunk and you whisk me
out of your apartment. I normally drive home
and write poetry on how I think you're oh-so-

beautiful and very smart. But I never show it to you because it's bloated and it sucks, like it was written by a crooning fifteen-year-old. It's normally about your lips and your brain. And how I could give two shits about your mole that all the other boys like—they say it reminds them of Cindy Crawford. You are innocence experienced, and all those other boys don't understand that the mole isn't the most uniquely beautiful thing about you—it's your voice, your voiceis full of music. Beautiful, but pointless, its only purpose to exist as beautiful, but pointless in the endless procession of the universe like everything is in the end. But without these little human eccentricities that make life beautiful, who would want to be anything at all?"

TRACK 6. **LYSANDER 7 - GIRLS**

You could act precocious, you could be ferocious
You can run away from me and hide
But I'm not gonna worry, I'm not in a hurry
You will come around to me in time, 'cause love is
everything that you need
It always comes back to love, kissin' and a-huggin'
is the air that I breathe
I'll always make time for love.

—"Don't make this about me!"

She yells in a whisper. Not quite crying, but you can see the thought crossed her mind.

—"I'm not! But you're part of it, and for you to think otherwise would be you lying to yourself. I'm not asking you to change me, just like I'm not asking you to change. If anything changed, then we wouldn't have those moments of irrevocable us-ness when we make those stupid little jokes no one else get, or when we kiss stupidly. I love that it's difficult for other people to be in the same room as us because we forget they're even there! It's then, then that we fucking rule."

—"I love you Daisy, and I know it, and I don't care if you don't, because this isn't going to change anytime soon."

She looks at me with big, sad eyes full of water, but I can't help myself. I jump on her, and we have passionate but gentle sex. We didn't bother putting on music. I kiss her neck as she breathes in my rhythm. My mind goes blank. I forget about writing, or dying young, or where she might be next week. I want time to stop, but life isn't fiction, so I kept kissing her neck, holding her shoulders. If time stopped, this moment wouldn't continue and I could never kiss the other side of her neck, or cup her breast in a different manner. She wouldn't continue to breathe and we couldn't listen to the music. I would never be able to set eyes on her for the first time of the day, or kiss her as I press against her hips. I let the thought pass and close my eyes. I continue to kiss her, listening to the music of her breath and believing in love.

DEAD?

Open your eyes. You are dead. Feel your face, it's okay. Touch the ground, you can't, it's okay. This is heaven. This is hell. This is purgatory. This is Route 66 on desolation row with the wind a blowin', and don't even think twice because it's all not alright.

She's gone. Not dead, gone, it's okay. Feel your face, you can't. She's better off, admit that: *she is better off.* Keep walking, walk away, just keep walking, one two, one two, one two. *It's okay.* You're dead, accept it.

Smile. You don't have to, but you might as well. Wave at JFK and Jackie O will smile like a donut. Take the drink, you don't have a schedule, it's okay. Why does it feel the same? Well that's quite a good question. Sit down.

It is the same. The way that life is life is the way that death is death, and you're dead, *it's okay.* Just stop talking, stop talking please. Okay, shut the fuck up! This is for your benefit. Is there a God you say? I thought I told you to shut the fuck up? No, no, it's okay. Is there a God? I don't know, you tell me. If there is and we are created in his image, don't you think vanity would compel him to let us know? So is there a God, no. There is no God. God is dead, like you, you're dead. Rise, converge, smile. Just smile. Wake up. No, I'm just fucking with you. You're awake, well at least as close to being awake as you can be, being dead and all. Keep walking. We're almost there. Yes, we're almost there. Well, as close to there as we can be. Are you daft? You're dead, no schedule, nowhere to go. And what's with the socks? You don't need socks, you actually don't need clothes. You don't need a body, and you don't need a wallet, so there's no point in pants, because there's no use for pockets. You're not really handling this well, are you? It's okay. Lose the pants, that's the first step.

I don't know if you're ready. Don't go getting excited, there's no alternative. Well actually there is an alternative. *It* requires me to tell you.

Your blue pill is the light switch. Yes, the light
switch on the wall. Well, it's sort of a wall, and
not really a light switch, but yes the light switch
is the alternative. What happens? Another good
question, I hate good questions. It's okay. It's okay.
Stop crying. Just stop.

Who am I? Hmm. Philosophical on the first
date. Next, you'll be going for boob. It's not important, like you, you're not important. You're not
a snowflake, or a panda, or a hibiscus. No roses for
you, and definitely no scones with your coffee.
No coffee at all. It's okay, you're dead. That's all.
Remember the light switch. Okay. It's okay. Let
it be okay.

SAN FRANCISCO:
AN AUTOBIOGRAPHY

DEAR SAN FRANCISCO,

Sliding chaotically down Portola from the outward spreading suburbs that are the Sunset, you
see San Francisco, beautiful, teeming with life,
luster, and loss. The only sight it can be compared
to is a woman lying naked, waiting, her eyes pull-
ing you towards her, your brain without thought.

San Francisco, I want you to be my mother.
I want desperately to have the right to say my
birthing origins occurred on your sacred grounds,
where I think there is absolutely everything. From
your famous fog to the fantastical sight of watching it swallow the Golden Gate Bridge, permeate
into every convex crevice that our maze of urba-

nia offers, I love you and promise never to break your heart.

MISSION

You are my favorite district from your international food perks to the vibrant chords of life that breathe through your mostly dirty streets, to the hip and happy bars that make me forget everything and everyone, crowded with beautiful hipster girls that I hate and love all at once—me too afraid, too enamored to subject myself to denial for their bubbles of desire floating in my mind's sky popping in and out of my everyday moments.

From taking the 49 and meeting the most kind and respectful meth addicts you'll ever have the pleasure of knowing who shoot up next to you in the back right corner of the bus at 11:43 on a Wednesday night, even sometimes asking for your permission first.

To the lives destroyed, souls sucked dry stumbling from instigation to instigation, screaming in front of the 24TH St. BART about god or the devil or anything in-between. Screaming to be heard and looked at because they have nothing else but a voice of pain and a cry of hopelessness.

Mission, you house my favorite bar in the city, where they let you smoke inside, and no one says anything about it. Everyone just acts like it's the 80's and pretty much all the music is from the 80's, and most of the people dress like they're in the 80's. I guess it's kinda like being in the 80's…I love places you can smoke inside. It feels so risky, like your parents are going to catch you at any second and for those 3-6 minutes depending what you're on (what substance and at what level/depth and while killing yourself over a lifetime) you feel the brief ecstasy (great name for a drug) of childhood. I refuse to release the name of the bar as it is small and crowded enough with hipster scum that I probably am too. I fucking hate waiting five minutes for a beer.

24TH may be my favorite street in the city. Nothing like walking down smelling carnitas (which I don't eat) and soaking in the magical murals of quasi-realism. You are sunny when nowhere else is, and walking down your street is perhaps the closest I will ever get to La Boca. You were there for me while I watched Barcelona win the champions league in my favorite taqueria in the city. I owe you.

If I could choose any district to be my secret ethnic hipster lover, you would be her. We would walk to Dolores Park and lay in the sun counting every remarkable thing we could see. We would drink beer and smoke pot and have conversations with bums and friends about feminism and *Young Frankenstein* and would argue in defense of our favorite Woody Allen films. Obviously, there is no other answer than "*Annie Hall.*" If you disagree, please don't tell me or anyone else because, sweetheart, you're wrong (pat on shoulder). And if we're just going to be open about trying to be cool, 'cause even (especially) the 40-year-olds are competing in the category of taste, it is necessary to mention Valencia, all bathed in hipster shame and glory. Valencia, you make me feel like I am in LA, which I secretly like, without you how else would I dreary eyed ogle the sassy pixie girls with feathers in their ears, hair, and, sometimes, their noses. You remind me of the detest I have accrued toward bikers—not the leather wearing kind. You are home to Boogaloo's, a wonderful place where the hip waitresses don't make you feel like a complete asshole for not knowing every lyric to the punk music blaring in the background.

Oh Mission, how grand it is to sit on the patio of El Rio on a sunny Thursday embracing the splendor of an undeserved happy hour. You and I, reveling in intoxication, stumbling back to my home (which is technically in Bernal Heights, a beautiful lesbian couple told me that) and innocently fool around before getting to the heavy stuff.

BERNAL HEIGHTS

My home. I love your streets and my coffee shop, the one run by a co-operative of lesbians who know the names of their patron's children. I adore and take for granted I can get food from five different continents (Americanized of course) within a one-block radius! You are the first place that has felt like home since I fell out of the parental nest, a scared little bird in a big new city, pretending to go to school. Then I stopped going to school to be a full-time writer, which means I need a day job; actually, I have a part-time night job. I wear a shit-eating grin, lie to foreigners, and sell over priced shrimp(s) to overweight Californians who don't know there's better cheap food mere blocks away. But I'll get to that later.

Bernal Heights, I love standing on your shoulders and looking at what should be the center of existence: San Francisco—its majestic natural beauty covered elegantly in a concrete blouse of urban jungle. Once, when I climbed to your peak, I saw little kids light the hill on fire with a fire cracker and run from the police. At first, the brush fire seemed like it was going to engulf the hill and achieve the horrible glory of a hillside with houses spectacularly ablaze. But the fire smoldered unspectacularly and failed to reach its potential. We're all fire; words are fire.

Bernal Heights: I never want to leave you; of course I'm going to occasionally cheat on you with the Mission and Haight, and there was a period of my life where I slept in North Beach almost every night. But you're my girl, my buddy, my muse. I never want to leave you, and even though I don't appreciate you like I should, you'll always know I love you.

OUTER MISSION

You kind of scare me, particularly around Geneva, but goddamn your Mexican food is so fucking good. Taqueria Guadalajara is the only burrito I've ever had that can hold a torch to Southern California's. I saw one of the most intriguing human exchanges ever in your hallows. An enormous man, the kind you ironically call "Tiny," walked in and started yelling at somebody hiding behind the counter, as I would have been had Tiny been chasing after me. It was 2:30 on a Saturday morning, everyone is drunk, really shit-faced, except for me (I was grass high as a fucking kite, but I wasn't drinking that often at this point in my life, at least nowhere near as much as I am now).

Anyhow as Tiny pushed his way through the crowded restaurant, he bumped particularly hard into a small Hispanic man in an olive green business suit. The counter at Guadalajara is L-shaped, Tiny is standing at the base of the L. The smaller man gathers himself and pushes Tiny over a bowl of oranges they always keep next to the water container at the base of the L. It was like something out of a cartoon. The whole restaurant sees what's happening.

As Tiny catches himself and drunkenly half-realizes what just happened, you see the fat rolls of his face (but not his eyes—he was wearing sunglasses—at 2:30 at night!) flush with embarrassment. He does what an Alpha does, wails on the smaller Hispanic man's face, everyone surrounding too scared to do anything: me, myself, and I included. After hitting the man in the face, and continuing to do so while the small man is on the ground, probably like 8 more times. Then the same look of flushed embarrassment overcomes him, and he runs (his version, anyway, of "run") out of the restaurant. The small man is lying on the ground, barely conscious, bleeding from his head. His family goes to him with a wad of napkins, which they put to his open head wound/ gash. The entire taqueria's eyes are transfixed on the poor small man and his small family, wondering if he's alive.

We hold our breaths collectively, everyone pretending we care, and maybe we do, but we're all secretly glad it's not us. Aw sweet Humanity! Then what feels like, but doesn't sound like, a collective gasp encompasses the entire restaurant. The man gets up, gives a small, pain filled smile, and everyone goes back to their business: drinking cerveza and eating Guadalajara's famous burritos—the small man and his family included. Then the police show up, and all the drunk (and stoned) eaters and drinkers miraculously forget anything happened at all. Maybe this never happened, and I'm just making it up, memory is a many splendored thing. Memory is everything. Without memory we would never exist, right?

BAYVIEW

I looked at a house here one time. The second I got there I immediately knew I didn't want the house. Okay, I'm spoiled, but I am willing to pay 200 more dollars per month to not live in a broken down industrial shithole. Other than that I've never been to Bayview.

One of my old roommates used to buy stuff for his pot plants there, like lights and vitamins. I heard there's a donut shop/bar combination that the guy from Girls goes too, Girls the figurehead of San Francisco's stellar music scene with lyrics so simple and clean, so full of reality that they hit hard. Chris (the lead singer)—your sweeping croon tickles my spine like the yellow fog of Prufrock lore. When I see you live—I can't keep this to myself anymore—I think your knee shuffles are adorable. I love that you used to have a guitarist that looked like the kid from "Dazed and Confused," you know the main one who hates Ben Affleck. Everyone should hate Ben Affleck. Your music has gotten me through some blue periods and attaches to the energy in my bloodstream during those sporadic periods when life genuinely excites me. The first time I saw you will be something I'll never forget, maybe the greatest show I've ever seen. My Fitzgerald moment of music, I'll get to that later.

It was Valentine's Day. My mom owns a flower shop in Santa Barbara. When you own a flower shop, Valentine's Day is the worst day of the year. Every year, I drive down there and help deliver flowers. It's one of the few times a year my entire immediate family spends together, irritated, exhausted, but fulfilling the obligations of familial love. I get off of work at 5 o'clock and drive to San Francisco, a six hour drive. Mind you I had been driving since 7am, and if you've never been a taxi driver, delivery boy, or gone on an extended road trip, you have no idea how painful driving can be. In my 15th hour of driving, I realize there is a Girls show at the Great American Music Hall. At this stage in my life, Girls was my favorite new band. At this stage in my life, I also had a crazily angry little Filipino girlfriend who looked far too good naked.

And when I say crazy, I don't mean like a frat boy saying a chick's crazy because she got angry after he fucked her best friend. I mean like, "one flew north, one flew west, one flew over the cuckoo's nest" crazy. Stupid things like holidays and birthdays meant a lot to her because of her incessant need to feel important. She wanted me to hang out with her, but I desperately wanted to go to the Girls show.

Driving past SFO (20 minutes out of the city), I see a white Subaru station-wagon fly past me with improvisational velocity. Moments later more police cars than I can count shoot past with an angry demeanor. How can inanimate objects have any demeanor? Just ask a tree, fauna's people.

Now I have a confession to make. It was one of coolest fucking things I've ever seen. Like watching "Cops" (the tv show) in person. The thing is, I hate action movies, and explosions, and

Transformers, to the point where if I go to one,
I will get absurdly stoned and fall asleep, wake
with the explosions, doze again—five, six times.
Thus I thought it was strange how this exam-
ple of speed greed affected me so heartily. That's
what my dad would do when I forced him to go
to these pieces of shit (action flicks) as a kid—
fall asleep. Hereditary procession, genetics: something inevitable.

This police chase at that time in my life was
a sign, a symbol. Go figure, guess it was the car
eluding the cops, exciting, brave? I needed to be
selfish and do something for me. I wanted out of
my relationship, but I was too scared to say anything, stuck in the depression of being 21, never
having another birthday to look forward to. That
was compounding with boredom, I was so goddamn life/relationship bored. It's true, you should
never date someone you can't talk to. Also she
would threaten to kill herself when I wasn't at-
tentive enough. Something that scared the piss
out of me, but after the 15th threat I just kinda
wanted to see if she would do it. I suppose that
would equivocate to, "I shot a man in Reno, just
to watch him die." The shady sides of the human

mind are dangerous places to hide when trying to get out of the sun of inundation.

I call her.

—"I'm too tired to hang out."

She freaks out, but this was a mild one. A 3.2 on the Richter scale of crazy.

I get to the show to find it's sold out. But after deciding to put myself out there, I begin asking strangers for extra tickets. I find a ticket for cheaper than door price. I go in. The GAMH has in's and out's. So fucking essential. I go to the bar pound 3 beers, then run to my car to smoke 3 bowls. The number 3 works wonderfully for compulsive addicts.

I go back in and Girls is just starting. They had flowers wrapped around their microphones, and balloons tied to the drum kit. They were all on cocaine and alluded to this with muffled subtlety. It was the best damn show I've ever seen. And it made me realize I didn't love the crazy girl that looked good naked. Thank you Girls, I love you.

And Bayview, how do you have so many police officers and still so many problems? You should be ashamed of yourself.

INGLESIDE

You need to be more interesting. Living in Ingleside is like staying at your Grandma's house for two weeks over the summer when you're seventeen. Everything stops at 8'clock, the food sucks (I will maintain always that cooking is not an Irish grandmother's strong suit—drinking, well that's a different story) and you're always horny because going out costs so fucking much because every night includes a 20-25 dollar cab ride home.

Ingleside, your hills are treacherous. I woke up every sacred drunken night I could sneak in at the age of 20 with bruises the size of soft balls on my legs and tears in my pants. You made me a stoner because there was nothing to do. You were where for a brief time in history I stopped writing, stopped reading, stopped giving a shit about anything—other than raves and soulless electro music.

Despite my open and outward disdain for you, you have held moments that are dear to me. And sometimes when the sun's out and you're on one of those treacherous hills, you have some of the most spectacular views this planet has to offer.

You are where I first tried so much, and where I made some friends that will be dear to me for life.

SFSU

Thank you for Michael Krasny (the man who helped me understand "The Wasteland"), and thank you pretty much the entire English department. That's where underpaid teachers are forced to take sabbaticals (budget crunch) and yet they still actually give a shit about the subject matter, and sometimes their students, the good ones at least. Thank you for cheap coffee and your intelligently laid out design.

But fuck you for charging me thousands of dollars more each semester and without even giving me the benefit of having a functioning library. Thank you for nursing my alcoholism with your perverse boredom and lack of beauty. Thank you for my freshman year of college, where I lived on your haunted grounds that can be best surmised in one drunken anecdote:

When I was 20 I was dating a short girl with a fast mouth and pretty blonde hair. At this time in my life I was drinking heavily, probably 5-7 times a week, not like a beer or two, but getting shitfaced. One of these nights where I remember nothing, I managed to stumble from her tiny traditional dorm room, replete with all the nominal college complacencies: band posters, 2 desks, and celebrations when her roommate would go home for the weekend allowing us to fuck freely.

On a particularly drunken Saturday, I stumble to her neighbor's door and mistake it for the bathroom. I remember none of this, but know it happened because I returned from my blackout with a little girl dressed in purple doing her best not to punch me. Screaming obscenities.

Now the purple shirt is essential because at San Francisco State University purple is the Resident Advisors' (College vernacular for what surmounts to be the Fun Police) uniforms, the purple police. This one happened to be the head resident advisor. You know she's that big a bitch when she schedules herself for the all night Saturday shift.

She is livid, white hot with anger. I am wearing nothing except for tiny Swedish boxer briefs, not even blessed with the benefit of shoes. Her voice shaking, she asks my name and where I live.

I'm still reasonably hammered in my clouded stupor, but I offer a fake answer.

—"Paul Rodriguez, 404 Mary Park."

Put that through a drunken voice modulator and that's more or less what I offered her. She delves deeper, more questions, something, something, something, sounding like a grown-up in Charlie Brown. She's doing all this to circumscribe the proper punishment to crawl and shape itself in my life.

It's beneficial to know at this point I was on probation for having got caught with illegal substances many, many times. I always had the good fortune to never get arrested, but this night felt like a night for new things.

Realizing this, I begin to sprint without shoes to the stairwell. Fortunately, my girl lived on the second floor. My building, "The Towers," was around 1000ft. or 330 meters away. I ran the thing like Michael fucking Johnson.

When I arrived at the front door, which you need a swipe card to open, which I obviously don't have as I don't store my valuables up my ass, though that's not the worst idea, at least you'd never lose shit (heh). There is no one at the desk, which was so goddamn fortunate for me. I pry the sliding doors open, run to my basement apartment, and quickly change into a makeshift outfit that was as mismatched as anyone who had the good fortune to live through the psychedelic decades.

At this point, it's around four in the morning, and I decide for some reason to return to my girlfriend's dorm. I see two of my best friends/roommates—liking your roommates is one of the greatest gifts bestowed on a 20-something. We exchange "What's ups." They're laughing already and in a joking manner they ask,

—"Have you seen a guy running around in his underwear?"

—"Dude, how did you know?"

—"A cop asked us if we saw a guy running around in his underwear."

—"That was fucking me."

They die with laughter as I scurry back to my girlfriend's dorm. A cop car's parked out front. As I walk in, the cop asks if I've seen a guy running around in his underwear. I pause, give him a disgusted look, and say of course not, then walk away. I walk up the stairs—to my surprise there are no cops around. The bitchy RA is standing in the lobby, her face flush red, yelling at the elevator to hurry the fuck up. I say hi, but she doesn't say hi back. My girlfriend, beautiful and half naked standing in her doorway down the hallway, motions for me to hurry my ass in.

SUNSET

I hate you. You're always foggy and you're worthless—ugly with suburban sprawl. Your cultural contribution to San Francisco can be surmised by a fart. If it weren't for Irving and Judah and Golden Gate Park, I would write a proposal for your nuclear bombing.

Your only saving grace that isn't kissing Golden Gate Park is the grotesque number of house parties you allow to exist. Oh yeah, and Shannon Arms has gotten the guy I'm in a bromance with a consistent "DJing" gig.

And don't even get me started on 19th street. Drive on that shit Labor Day weekend, but only if you're a masochist.

GOLDEN GATE PARK

Thank you. Your museums are a gift to culture and your beauty decadent, but irrepressible, contagious. You are the home for Outside Lands, which is the reason I wrote "White Lights," probably the first piece of quasi-fiction I have ever written.

You are the first place I tried acid. And when I finally did get to go to Outside Lands, it was as good as I expected, which is so exceptionally rare, with how increasingly jaded and cynical I've become. I think they call that getting older?

While on age, when did 15-year-olds start looking so young? I remember the few people I still know from when I was 15 being 15 and not looking anywhere as young as they do now. And then once they hit 23, you can't tell how old they are until you hit 35, and your posture starts to droop because gravity is heavy, and without it we couldn't stay grounded, and we'd all float away like Remedios, how poetically beautiful and tragic.

One time my former manager and current friend (shit, I forgot to call on his birthday) who was exceptionally good at guessing peoples ages told me,

—"You can't look at the face, you have to look in the eyes."

And when I stop and think about it, it really is amazing how much of somebody's soul exists in the eyes. If you look them straight in the pupils, and don't lie to yourself, you can tell absolutely everything about someone without speaking. Ariel Pink (another one of LA's strong suits) was wrong, you can hear my eyes.

You have buffalos, and beautiful tree people that let me observe them extensively and watch over the world breathing while I'm on acid having my private and silent conversations with nature. Then lying on my back and asking questions to the expansive sky painted in its vibrant twilight, a still life Van Gogh in real time, realizing how amazing the song Fireworks is. Possibly the best of 00's.

I've played soccer in you maybe half a dozen times. You are the closest thing to Never Never Land I've ever had the pleasure of knowing.

HAIGHT

As cool as it would be to hate you because you're so goddamn chic and popular, I can't, you're simply too wonderful. You are rich with hippie history and blended with a movement that formed the freethinking worthlessness of my generation. You have edgy boutiques that are unique along with countless head shops that are pretty much all the same. I dare you to walk down Haight and not see a beautiful girl (usually with a beautiful boy). It's like licking your own crotch, (almost) impossible.

You are the home of the first girl I ever fell in love with in the city. The first girl that broke my heart and jarred me from the sleepy stoner stagnancy that infected me in my early 20's. In her apartment, which was pure LA, we had conversations that were exciting

—Her: Modest Mouse is probably the best band ever.

—Me: I personally don't consider cocaine a drug.

—Me: 'Oh, no! Do you believe in God?'

—Her: 'I believe in energy.'

—Her: Excuse me for pontificating but I think you're in love with the idea of me.

—Me: I don't know if I believe in love.

We'd sit and talk like that through the night, her across from me, beautiful. If I weren't so proud I'd tell her I miss her.

You have some wonderful bars, and have housed so many house shows that have welcomed my company. One of the five best breakfasts of my life happened on Haight, at All you Kneed where my friend told me the girl would break my heart but the eggs benedict and conversation were so damn good I didn't care even though I knew he was right. His name's Carrey, I love him, he's the one I'm in a bromance with.

Lastly, I know if I ever need to get a quick tattoo or redo my Prince Albert piercing (Look it up. Warning: Must be 18 or older) you'll be there; you'll be there. Oh yeah, Buena Vista Park is absolutely gorgeous. Oh yeah, homeless people, lots of 'em. Thank you for keeping them out of the Mission, or at least evening the spread.

PANHANDLE

I love you because of your sunny days and for your having trees and grass and birds. For giving my two favorite girls in the city their more than comfortable apartments. The two young women are both dynamic conversationalists and easy to look at. One, the one I fell in love with whom I said lives in the Haight, actually she says she lives in the Panhandle (or if you really wanna be a snob, NOPA), because it's cleaner—she's from LA. Her best friend lives within walking distance of her serene Green and White apartment, her friend's apartment is just as serenely white. She makes you take your shoes off. If you forget she berates you for getting her fuzzy white carpet dirty, the same carpet we rub our faces on when we're rolling.

Cheers to the musings we've exchanged when we're stoned. And salud to what I remember when I write about it, because sometimes it's genuinely poignant. It's beautiful and rare to have a poignant conversation with someone, hold onto them and do whatever it takes to keep them in your life.

Thanks to the girl that inspired me to write again (at first, I was trying to impress her, but to impress someone you must first impress yourself). Ode to the first time I ever saw her and "All Shook Up" became my favorite song (for the week). I temporarily believed in love again. And I feel no shame whatsoever in admitting that everything I've ever written is because of that girl (and maybe a few others). Just read "Araby"— everything ever written, sung, or stroked is because of a girl, is for a girl—unless it's for a boy. We're all just fish swimming in a bowl trying to get fucked. And you don't even have to apologize for the broken heart, and how I picked up the pieces, put them up my nose because of the writing you inspired. Inspiration is much less common than a broken heart.

Oh, and your taste (and your taste!) in music is super hot. One time you asked what my type is, or maybe I asked you, but I said you weren't my type. I lied. My type is any beautiful hipster girl who knows who Neutral Milk Hotel is. The Cindy Crawford mole doesn't hurt and your intonation makes me feel like I did in 4th grade when my blazingly hot teacher refused to wear her bra, which prematurely urged my best friend and I to start puberty.

And to Ballz (the other beautiful girl), I never thought you would be as awesome as you are. You two together are great, please stay raving cocaine Feminists and never deny your love for each other. If you fight, kiss and make up, and let me watch.

RICHMOND

I have very little experience with you. I suppose I owe you for providing her coke dealer with a home. Oh yeah, and when I got kicked out of campus housing my freshman year of school, I was supposed to live with an old stoner lady my dad knows. She oozes sex despite being 63. If I were 63, I would fuck her, but I'm not (maybe never will be) and my mom kept telling me she was a cougar, which scared the shit out of me. My parents ended up giving her a large amount of money for a room that I never went to because no one ever came to evict me at the dorm. Even though it was "illegal" for me to be in the building, I stayed—the cougar lady scared me. Oh also I hear you have good Thai food, and that it's super easy to get laid at 550 Club on Mondays—is that true? I did have a transcendental experience driving down Geary one day. I'm fairly certain I was on my way to score cocaine (I was). Driving down your streets, I was wearing my unassuming little black frame glasses. I could see for miles, which in the city is a rare treat. Driving down San Francisco's main arteries, a miracle happened—every light was green. It was like *Meet the Fockers,* but it didn't end up sucking. That night I was going to hang out with the girl I fell like a leaf for, who lived in the Panhandle (Haight). Whenever I knew I was going to hang out with her, I got that feeling, the one where your stomach feels like millions of little people are dancing—Electric Daisy Carnival Jay's stomach. You get all antsy and time moves at a distorted pace, impossibly slow, then disjointingly fast. You shoot into your brain to create memories that will never exist, practicing conversations, looks, and ways to kiss her in a non-awkward fashion. I'd store away several talking points and pray I'd remember them in case things go awkward. But things rarely get awkward on cocaine; only falsely important, and teen drama dramatic.

I remember thinking everything was in front of me. On the road I was finally going at the right pace. Maybe ambition was slowly fading, but what was truly important to me was at my fingertips or a phone call away. I remember the innocent jubilance of seeing something that thousands had seen before, but was something I'd maybe never see again. Green light, after green light, after green light. An affirmation of acceptance and everything being right in the world: a symbol. Life is full of symbols but is desperately lacking interpretation. The way these symbols are (or are not) interpreted make us who we are. Do we lie to ourselves, are we irritatingly cynical, or are we positive balls of energy desperate for connection and exchange? Desperate to create and live, a mad one(s)—I've been a mad one before, I've also been a sad one. Right now I languish in the between.

MARINA

You are so detestably bogey. I never go here, but I hear some of the younger Giants party out there, a certain pot smoking Cy-young winner. Also, holy shit, so many hot women! You are another aspect of San Francisco that reminds me of LA.— one of Southern California's minimal strong suits, large amounts of exceptionally sculpted women.

My broman's favorite restaurant in the city is Osha Thai, which he's right about: it is better

in the Marina than at their sub-par satellite loca-
tions. One time I saw a play at the Magic Theater,
"Word for Word," Thomas Wolfe, it was pretty
exceptional. The girl that played the daughter in
one of the stories was effervescently dreamboatish,
and in my high stupor I convinced myself she was
in love with me like I was with her, at least for the
duration of the performance.

Also I would sacrifice a testicle to scientific
research for a house on Marina Blvd. Impossibly
gorgeous on a sunny day, with the dense cor-
respondence of life proceeding on your grassy
shores, kites flying and everything in life that's
good and nubile.

FISHERMAN'S WHARF (MORE SPECIFICALLY PIER 39)

If you ever catch on fire, I want to stand at a
safe distance with my glasses on, the ones I never
wear, and watch. I want a lawn chair, a six-pack
of artisan beer, and a full pack of Camel Filters.
I want to sit there next to six beautiful naked
women and watch. You have played the largest
part of any in the ever continuing destruction of
my soul. You are where I work.

—"My name's Jay, and I am a (I'll be your) waiter."

I have been demeaned by fathers in front of their entire extended family, second, even third cousins included. I have been condescended to by people who can't spell the word 'people.' I have learned that -isms still exists. Racism, classism, sexism, not to mention ignorance, in the minds of the larger percentage of Americans, Americans who don't know or even care that LBJ signed the Civil Rights Act in 1964. That in 1964 as a nation our country did something ten years before un-thinkable. That we finally turned progressive thought (once transgressive) into law. And I am reminded how far we have to go when I hear drunk people make the same damn joke about how many gay people live in San Francisco. That if I say something salted with even the slightest touch of innuendo they will make that joke, and I'll look at them and smile while thinking what disgusting pieces of shit they are. I know because I work at a restaurant that requires me to men-tion trivia about a movie that I hate.

I smile for tips. Sometimes when I'm at work, when it's slow and I'm high, I think about how absurd it all is. How wasteful this "tradition" is:

Going to a place that throws out enough food to feed Calcutta, waiting for the food at a table in a room full of strangers, and stressing out about a waiter you assume is an idiot. And the pressure of it all because it involves money. All the goddamn pressures of money. When you have it, when you lose it, when you start caring about it, and it becomes the most important thing in existence because without it how are you going to go to a fried seafood restaurant with a theme, and pay much too much money for food that is scientifically proven to kill you.

Then some days when I wake up early and still drunk, and the still drunk careens with me to work—it seems worth it. Worth it for all the wonderful people I meet momentarily and the friends I've made at work. Worth it for how much I've learned about people. The beautiful Australian families so full of love it feels like a Hallmark Thanksgiving. Where the kid almost cried when they left because he realized he would never see me again, a lesson that can be quite difficult to accept when learned too young. To the two proposals of marriage I've seen, at my table, a yes and a no—never forgetting the man's face when she said no. And who could ever forget the mother fucker who barely spoke English (though he was born, raised, and will die in America) who managed to utter a discordant sentence of intellectual condescension in the form of "How fucking stupid can you be?" Possibly the only sentence not pidginized to idiot speak he uttered all night. And how I couldn't tell him to fuck himself, despite it being in the worst interest of my own personal safety, because I was working, and I had to quite properly tell him that I didn't appreciate his comment. And oh how desperately I wanted to reach across the table and grab his throat and scream to him that if he even understood how much human bullshit I had to swallow he'd throw a parade in my honor, but didn't—I needed money.

That's life, it's good it's bad, and it can't be perfect, it shouldn't be perfect and we're all so caught up in minutia distresses that we forget to take a second and count every beautiful thing that we can. We forget that no one knows why the fuck we're here; that we're all just floating in space, and breathing is a privilege, not a right.

Don't forget to see the seals.

NORTH BEACH

You are the reason I moved to San Francisco. You are the Beats, you are delicious, you are everything the world should be and more. From Washington Square to Café Trieste, and who could forget City Lights, the world's second favorite bookstore. My second favorite in the city.

Cheers to Vesuvio's where they obviously understand the hardships of the poor alcoholic by offering the recession special, a whiskey and a beer for four bucks. I love your gloomy, glory-filled rooms, your wicker chairs, and the random conversations I've stumbled into with the right amount of substance intake. One night myself and three other patrons discovered we all had the same professor: me in my 20's, him in his 40's, she in her 30's, the teacher educating generations. And we cheered and thanked him and agreed that educators should be paid better, but did nothing about it because one person can't make a difference, not without shitloads and shitloads of money.

Toast to Mama's where I had the best break-fast of my life. It was just my dad and I—I was 10. I ordered a waffle with strawberries and whip cream. Why do you have to be so damn good, with your line always around the block and your closing time at 3, I never get to eat you, but I will always remember the best breakfast of my life, where nothing extraordinary happened. No epiphany or life changing conversation, just a 10-year-old boy and his dad, going to a baseball game in the afternoon, staying up late and waking up early.

You're where I take girls when I'm trying to impress them, because of the regurgitated facts I can throw out, all learned from my dad. About how Kerouac used to walk your hallowed streets and Francis Ford Coppola wrote the screenplay for "The Godfather" there and blah blah blah. Word vomit, the things we do to get laid.

If you were a woman you would be a bangin' hot older hipster cougar sugar mama. I would sleep in your opulence while you smoked cigarettes using a quellazaire (think Cruella Deville). You would say crazy shit that I absolutely loved and thought was brilliant, me enraptured in naïveté, and I would feel touched by God to have been chosen by you. Then you would hit 50 and me 30 or your husband or numerous other lovers would find out about us. And I would get over it because the crows feet started walking across your face. You'd go insane and I would do my best to forget that you ever existed, like every other girl I've ever dated.

Oh North Beach, I sing of thee, if only you weren't so damn expensive and habitating your rich grounds was a possibility.

NOB HILL

I have very little experience with you. However, there are some experiences I am exceptionally fond of. You are home to the 24TH story pent–house we use to party at till 6 in the morning. The way 20 something's get access to a 24TH story penthouse is they have one friend who is insanely rich and gives no fucks about anything, especially the state of her parents' house when they see it in the morning. Anyway she is in love with your best friend and will do anything he asks. So she lets him have parties where you drink or snort molly, or do both.

At one of these parties we all took some OC and had a cuddle puddle, taking pictures. Then the girl whose penthouse it is takes three

too many and stops breathing and starts turning blue. Then you have to call the paramedics.
There are few things more shameful than having
to tell the paramedics what drugs you're on as
they do their best to resuscitate your blue friend.
You praying to the God you don't believe in that
she will come to and everything will be normal.
You bite your teeth and scream in your brain that
you hope this turns out better than the ending of
Requiem. It did, she was fine, she did break a rib
as our friend gave her CPR trying desperately
to sacrifice some of her own life into the blue
one to bring her back from the ever extending
void. Fucked up people helping more fucked up
people, Irelands National Anthem.

I remember the beauty of watching my friend
cry her name, scared out of his fucking mind she
was going to die, him holding her, the look on
his face, perhaps the best expression of compas-
sion I've ever witnessed. It's beautiful to be one of
humanity's witnesses.

Then the next day when Ballz and I were
driving I had to pull over and puke. I pulled over
in front of a Catholic school, business men with
their briefcases walking by. Neon yellow bile
shooting out of my mouth my stomach turning

my brain making a mental note to never do opiates again, then making a mental note to forget to never to do opiates again.

Nob Hill you also hold the hotel we got kicked out of two nights in a row, on one of those rolly weekends filled with the electro parties I detest out of one side of my mouth, yet take molly with the other. My excuse is I love getting fucked up. My friend, drug angel, former roommate, rented a hotel for a weekend of particularly good electro. We got back after the show, 50 of us in the Frank Sinatra suite. Smoking, drinking, snorting, screaming. The security guards come, they kick us out. We come back the next night, the same thing happens. I can't believe they let us go back, I can completely believe we got kicked out again.

Nob Hill, I have no feelings whatsoever towards you, but goddamn if you haven't supplied me with some wasteful and dangerous fun.

FINANCIAL DISTRICT

I have no experience with you. I used to walk through you to get to the BART when I would sleep at my friend's house in North Beach. I am astonished at how good looking some of the people are in business suits. It makes me wonder were they smart enough to deserve the amount of money they make or was it their jawline that got them their degree and charmed their interviewer? I'll never know, which I am exceedingly jealous of and exceptionally grateful for. I think how different my life would be if my eyebrows were a shade shapelier or my chin broad bold and beautiful. I wouldn't be me.

My head turns toward BART two blocks away, passing Starbucks on both sides of the street, the novelty Wells Fargo display and gourmet lunch places geared towards convenience and expedience. I love standing below the buildings touching the sky. Looking up, the buildings bending like a mirage. The windows at night with their little lights and smaller people. People working all night to put their kids through college. And the higher up the light, the higher up the person, at night most of the lights are in the middle of the building. Another looker flies by, taking my eyes with her, like they're on strings connected to her butt. I get to the BART more hungover than a 19-year-old that goes to San Diego State and do my best not to fall asleep, my abode a mere five stops or seven minutes away.

TENDERLOIN

I love your story, whether fiction or not, of how you got your name. Purportedly cops would get paid more for working the Tenderloin beat because of how dangerous it was. And with the extra cash they could afford better cuts of meat for their families. What a wonderful name for a district. How could a place dubbed the Tenderloin not be dangerous? Is the tenderloin dangerous? Kinda. Oodles and oodles of crack heads, hanging from every corner.

One drunken night, I was stumbling down Jones when a crack head popped out of the woodwork and offered to babysit my children. I was 19, didn't have any kids. He told me he would do a great job and that he had a shotgun. Needless to say I was scared, and he didn't get the job. This same night while waiting for the OWL, the 91, which is a bus that does a loop around the entire city, takes forever to get where you need to go, and has some of the most ridiculous vignettes of the human condition a person will ever see, I met the nicest crack head on the face of the Earth. If there were a crack head yearbook, he would win the male award for nicest crack head. Anyway, he comes up to me and asks for money; I asked him what he needed it for. He was dismissive and tried to change the subject. After prying for several more moments, he finally told me he'd been awake and on crack for the past three days. The way he said it was borderline adorable. He said it like a child admitting to some menial act of ill discipline which they know will yield minimal repercussions. He then asked for advice on how to get more money to get more crack. I told him to be honest and clean, probably the best job advice I've ever gotten or given.

POLK ST.

You hardly deserve your own section, but... I have a love/hate relationship with you. You're like a beautiful girl/guy with no personality, a waste of space but somehow I continue to stare and always go back. Your bars are impossibly packed on the weekends—they might as well serve deli style:

—"order 203, apple martini…"

But so many gorgeous girls, hip crowds, so much money talk and who's who and what the fuck—having a bad time is nearly impossible.

One night Carey and I were with our friend Jenna who has a Skrillex (who doesn't) haircut. Her friends from Reno were in town. People from Reno love to fucking party. We had drinks, then more drinks at their hotel. We were on our way to Polk St. We needed a cab, a task and a half for 11 people. One of the impossibly drunk Reno boys was standing in the bed of a pizza delivery truck. The pizza man came out, which I thought would result in a strange interaction. However, the kid convinced the pizza man to drive all 11 of us in his two-seater truck. Three in the cab, eight in the bed, me and Carey in the caboose, both of us holding on to the bed's door for dear life. It was impossibly stupid, and so much goddamn fun. Why are the dumbest things always so much fun? We made it to Polk safely and indulged in a night of decadent drinking and DJ bashing.

UNION SQUARE

Okay, I have a confession to make. Every fiber of my consciousness knows I should resent, even detest you. I don't. I love hopping on BART, popping out at Powell and walking along your crowded corridors, sashaying into H&M and buying cheap fashionable clothes. Then window-shopping at Urban Outfitters, mocking the patrons for how utterly hard they are trying to be hip, they doing the exact same thing to me. Checking prices on things I'll never be able to afford; why is being cool so expensive?

I love your heart-shaped apples, and sitting in your direct center with my dad wearing a hat like Raol Duke (*FEAR AND LOATHING*, PAUL!), but speaking to me like Hunter at his best. He says:

—"Jay, it's time to grow up, we're not paying for school anymore, you're on your own. I'm sorry, but you took too long."

I tell him I understand, I know, and thank him. Growing up is goddamned difficult. How do you make the transition? We're all just birds, and our parents have to drop us out of the nest so we can learn how to fly, guess we should probably drink less.

Walking to my favorite coffee shop (the lesbian one in Bernal Heights), I fixate on one of my favorite anecdotes about Fitzgerald.

Fitzgerald, in a car with his friends in his 20's. I think there were some women and booze of course. Riding in the sun in the back of a convertible; a realization undeniable overcame him. He thought to himself,

—"This is and will always be the greatest moment of my life."

His mind wailing with thoughts of nothing else to ever look forward to again (something like this happens in "This Side of Paradise"). Of course he was wrong, but that thought sometimes usurps my general disposition and transfixes me. Occasionally I am worried I am experiencing a Fitzgerald moment.

This moment represents the death of nubile innocence and the loss of lust for life. And while walking to the coffee shop, I realize this is the moment where one grows up. I still hope that never hits me for real. I'd rather be Peter Pan than Captain Hook, at least Peter can switch hands when he wants to masturbate.

SOMA

I love your name. If you were a girl, you're the kind I'd want to snort things off of. I would love to live in one of your chic modern lofts. I'm afraid that's gonna be a forever dream—money. You are home to my favorite nightclub where I have done so many goddamn drugs that I've fooled myself into believing I liked techno. A club which is basically a rave, but smaller and 21+ with beautiful women, beautiful men, over priced drinks, five rooms of mayhem.

You are the parent of 6TH street, the second most ghetto place I've ever seen. The first being a tent city in Los Angeles' infamous skid row, not far from the absolute beauty of the LA Flower Market. 6TH street has a needle exchange; I had no idea that needle exchanges existed in the United States, that's such a Netherlands thing. Probably the epitome of how fucking liberal San Francisco is. I love it. My old roommate said he saw a man leaning up against a telephone pole taking a shit at 8 in the morning in broad daylight. It's fragments of life and sights such as these that make me smile and make all the pressure of everything worth anything at all.

Other than that you're overrated. Oh The End Up is pretty cool—an after-hours club where you can do drugs out in the open and pretty much everyone just pretends not to notice. Is that a good thing?

MARKET ST.

San Francisco's dorsal aorta. You are the city. Encompassing everything beautiful and terrible. Touching every shade of life that exists in your consecrated terra firma. Ode to the F train, Ode to the Ferry building. Ode to all the life that permeates through your spirit inanimate. Ode to you and just you. All of you, the patter of your thousands of feet, the beating of your happy and sad hearts, your ever extinguishing life breath that gives value and poignancy to everything, even to Death our beautiful mother.

To the crack heads, who are dear to me, to the beautiful business ladies that turn their noses up when they see my unshaven face ogle them like a construction worker. To the 10's of millions of souls that have taken in your outrageous beauty. Market you are San Francisco and I love you. I wish I could kiss your feet and thank you for my habitation, cheers darlin', you're beautiful.

CASTRO

Your infamy precedes your greatness. You're famous enough for a Simpson's joke. Every time I go to Q-bar on a Monday, my life is ruined, but only in slight. Marcello's has arguably the best pizza in the city, which isn't saying much as San Francisco is a sandwich town. I don't remember anything from drunk and hung over Mondays, but have ascertained from my friends that sometimes I scream, laughing to myself and tear down dozens of posters advertising shitty summer action movies or big titties that everyone is supposed to like.

And sometimes when I'm sad about that girl, you know the one that still lives in the Haight (Panhandle), I go to your nightclubs and make out with lesbians and sometimes gay dudes. Then when I tell people they say they didn't know I was gay, and I try to tell them I'm not, I'm just okay with making out with dudes. I could never suck dick, but they just don't understand that one action (or four) does not define sexuality.

And why the stigmatization of homosexuals? There isn't enough money for social security anyway, so they're doing us all a favor by not having kids. Does it really make you that uncomfortable to see two dudes making out, or does it make your dick wiggle and that scares you? Are you intimidated by the fact that most gay dudes could beat the shit out of you, whilst their couture bag is slung securely over their left shoulder? Or are you jealous of all the beautiful women incessantly surrounding said gay dudes. The reason you're scared is because you've been culturalized to insinuate perversion from homosexuality. Isn't it tough enough that we're all in a desperate struggle to continue the eternal pathos of existence?

How many times have you seen two male dogs bang each other with that stupid happy and serene look on their face? Being gay rules, I just wish I were included.

DOLORES PARK

It's impossible to describe the ecstasy of drinking a Blue Moon and laying on your back shirtless on those rare sunny days in San Francisco. I
don't care how grimy your meanderers are, or the
constant possibility of seeing some dude with his
cock hanging out in broad daylight. The energy
that you let off is too beautiful to be denied. The
only thing that could even be considered a negative about your vivacious greatness would be
how long one has to wait for the bathroom. But
sometimes holding it feels good.

   I have to extend genuine thanks for giving
me a conversation I'll remember forever with the
lost and maybe gone forever Haight girl and her
beautiful friend who both have beautiful brains.
How we talked and argued and laughed about
Exit Through the Gift Shop. Then Feminism. Then
both of them in their relation to each other. At
the time I was reading Martin Eden, but I hadn't
finished it yet, but I wish I had because how elegantly he explains art and its relation to the critics who create the cannon and how one critic
can change your life, make you or destroy you.
And people only like what they're told to like,

that taste isn't objective anymore and that taste is related to intelligence. So if you can convince people you're smarter than they are they'll like what you like. And intelligence isn't objective either, but how can creativity be subjective? It's finite proof that critics and hipsters are all failed artists. They refuse to be honest with themselves, espousing bullshit and refusing to admit when they are called out on it. Brainwashed taste-Nazis.

We couldn't quite understand what we were saying, but we were so close, and stoned, and a little bit drunk that it vibrated in our souls like a perfectly placed minor chord. Then the guy on LSD came up to us and he was perfect too, then we left and these black dudes smoking a blunt while driving started hitting on my (pretty) girls, but they were perfect too because sometimes life is undeniable.

Your heralded movie nights that I've never attended. The acid trip that hasn't happened yet. Your view. Oh my fucking god, your view. Possibly the greatest thing ever. Isn't it funny that humans will do almost anything to get a good view, from climb a mountain to eating at a shit restaurant? Views are music for the eyes.

NOE VALLEY

Another one of the places draped in luxury. Noe Valley your early 30's professionals with dogs and babies make me sick. A not so subtle reminder of the success I will never achieve. Your entire district is basically that fucking guy who puts on spandex, wakes up at 6 in the morning on a Sunday, and jogs a 5k. And sometimes when I'm still awake from the night before probably rolling my dick off or coked out of my mind I want to stop him. Then ask him to stop listening to the Dave Matthews Band or Toad the Wet Sprocket and scream "What the fuck are you doing! For god sakes enjoy your life once in a while!" What's the point of living forever if you never have fun?

It deserves a mention that the most put to-gether person I've ever dated was born and raised in Noe Valley. She was beautiful and brilliant, and 20 with a college degree in psychology. And sometimes she would look at me with rhapsodic desire that would turn the lower half of my body to liquid butter. Then one night I got way too drunk, as I always do, and she saw the other end of my potential. The one that ends with me face down in a gutter drowning on my own vomit. A bottle in my hand and my only regret that I won't be able to drink tomorrow. What she saw in me I'll never know, but she was the kinda girl you absolutely marry if she'll let you. I really fucked that one up, if I had a nickel for every time I said that, I'd have 15 cents.

BERNAL HEIGHTS

A cab ride, another far-too-long night, and I'm home. I hope I wake up before noon.

SAN FRANCISCO

Seven miles wide, seven miles long. My life exists within 49 square miles and in no way do I feel like anything is lacking. I am home. Feeling at home is so damn comforting, it makes all my other problems small: the drinking, the lack of balance, the loss of love, and the back and forth of my luster dwindling and amplifying. But I can't complain because I am alive, and I have a place to sleep. I could be doing much worse, and much better. I hope it's always that way because perfection is boring and everyone should always have a goal. San Francisco, Bernal Heights, the Mission, North Beach, and all other districts: I love you. Please always change, but in the same manner as you continue to be. XX (and not the band).

LOVE,
JAY

ABOUT THE AUTHOR

Joe Riley is a native Californian, a graduate of SFSU, and, as his short story *San Francisco: An Autobiography*, illustrates, he now lives, writes, and works in San Francisco. When not writing songs for various garage bands in his adopted City of Lights, he is completing work on a romantic novella and a novel.

COLOPHON

The text of this book is set in the stately Bembo, which finds its origins in the 15th century. Francesco Griffo cut a new typeface to typeset a relatively insignificant essay by the Italian scholar Pietro Bembo. There have been many revivals of Bembo in the last hundred years. The Monotype Corporation is very keen on preserving this harmonious and easy-to-read typeface, and to them humanity owes much gratitude.

Titles are set in Avenir, a linear sans designed by Adrian Frutiger in 1988.

This book was laid out in Adobe InDesign CS5 on a 2.53 GHz Intel Core 2 Duo MacBook Pro, running OS X Lion. This particular edition was produced by CreateSpace, an on-demand publishing company in San Luis Obispo, California.

Made in the USA
San Bernardino, CA
19 April 2013

2426082R00107